Enthusiastic Praise for
Barbara Delinsky

"One of today's quintessential authors of
contemporary fiction...Ms. Delinsky is a joy to
read. With the incisive skill of a surgeon and the
delicate insight of true compassion, she deeply
probes the quality and meaning of life....
Women's fiction at its very finest."

—*Romantic Times*

"[An author] of sensitivity and style."

—*Publishers Weekly*

"Ms. Delinsky has a special knack for zeroing in on
the pulse of her characters immediately—we know
them and understand what makes them tick within
the first few pages.... Well done!"

—*Rendezvous*

"When you care enough to read the very best, the
name of Barbara Delinsky should come immediately
to mind.... One of the few writers...who still writes
a great love story, Ms. Delinsky is truly an author for
all seasons."

—*Rave Reviews*

Barbara DELINSKY

THE REAL THING

Harlequin Books

TORONTO • NEW YORK • LONDON
AMSTERDAM • PARIS • SYDNEY • HAMBURG
STOCKHOLM • ATHENS • TOKYO • MILAN
MADRID • WARSAW • BUDAPEST • AUCKLAND

HARLEQUIN BOOKS

THE REAL THING

Copyright © 1986 by Barbara Delinsky

All rights reserved. Except for use in any review, the reproduction or utilization of this work in whole or in part in any form by any electronic, mechanical or other means, now known or hereafter invented, including xerography, photocopying and recording, or in any information storage or retrieval system, is forbidden without the written permission of the publisher, Harlequin Enterprises Limited, 225 Duncan Mill Road, Don Mills, Ontario, Canada M3B 3K9.

ISBN: 0-373-83277-X

First Harlequin Books printing November 1986

Reprinted January 1994

All characters in this book have no existence outside the imagination of the author and have no relation whatsoever to anyone bearing the same name or names. They are not even distantly inspired by any individual known or unknown to the author, and all incidents are pure invention.

This edition published by arrangement with Harlequin Enterprises B. V.

® and TM are trademarks of the publisher. Trademarks indicated with ® are registered in the United States Patent and Trademark Office, the Canadian Trade Marks Office and in other countries.

Printed in U.S.A.

Barbara Delinsky was born and raised in suburban Boston. She worked as a researcher, photographer and reporter before turning to writing full-time in 1980. With more than fifty novels to her credit, she is truly one of the shining stars of contemporary romance fiction!

This talented author has received numerous awards and honors, and her books regularly appear on the bestseller lists. With over twelve million copies in print worldwide, Barbara has truly universal appeal!

1

IT WASN'T EARTH-SHATTERING in the overall scheme of things. Nor was it unexpected. Yet coming as it did topping six weeks' worth of unpleasantness, it was the final straw.

Neil Hersey glared out the window of his office. He saw neither Constitution Plaza below him, nor anything else of downtown Hartford. The anger that blinded him would have spilled into his voice had not frustration already staked its claim there.

"Okay, Bob. Let me have it. We've been friends for too long to beat around the bush." He kept his fists anchored in the pockets of his tailored slacks. "It's not just a question of preferring someone else. We both know I'm as qualified for the job as any man. And we both know that Ryoden's been courting me for the past year. For some reason there's been an eleventh-hour reversal." Very slowly he turned. "I have my suspicions. Confirm them."

Robert Balkan, executive vice president of the Ryoden Manufacturing conglomerate, eyed the ramrod-straight figure across from him. He and Neil Hersey went back a long way. Their friendship was based on mutual admiration and genuine affection, and Bob respected Neil far too much to lie.

"Word came directly from Wittnauer-Douglass," he stated defeatedly. "Your release as corporate counsel there was a compassionate move. It was either let you go or bring you to trial."

Neil swore softly and bowed his head. "Go on."

"They alleged you were responsible for some transactions that were unethical, some that were downright illegal. For your own protection, the details remain private. The corporation is taking internal measures to counter the damage."

"I'll bet."

"What can I say, Neil? The charge was totally unsubstantiated, but it was enough to get the chairman of our board up in arms. One word in the old coot's ear and it became a crusade with him. Someone at Wittnauer-Douglass knew exactly what he was doing when he made that call. Then Ned Fallenworth got in on the act and that was that."

Fallenworth was the president of Ryoden. Bob had had reason to regret that fact in the past, but never as vehemently as he did now. "I've been spitting bullets since Ned gave me his decision. Ned's always been a coward, and what he's doing is a sad reflection on Ryoden. I gave it all I had, but his mind was closed. Narrow minds, Neil. That's what we're dealing with. Narrow minds."

Neil deliberately unclenched his jaw. "Narrow minds with a hell of a lot of power" was his own bleak assessment of the situation.

Leaving the window, he prowled the room, moving from parquet floor to Oriental rug and back, continuing the circle until he reached his gleaming mahogany desk. He leaned against the edge, his long legs extended and crossed at the ankles. His arms were folded over his chest. The pose might have been one of casual confidence under other circumstances. "Six weeks, Bob," he gritted. "This hell's being going on for six weeks. I'm being blackballed and it's touched every blessed aspect of my life. Something's got to give!"

"Do you need money? If it's a question of finances, I'd be glad to—"

"No, no." Neil waved aside the suggestion, then gentled his expression into a half smile of thanks. "Money's no problem. Not for now, at least." With the measured breath he took, the remnants of his half smile vanished. "The way things stand, though," he resumed, unable to stem his irritation, "my future as a lawyer in this town is just about nil, which is exactly what Wittnauer-Douglass intended."

"I think you should sue."

"Are you kidding?" Straightening his arms, he gripped the edge of the desk on either side of his lean hips. "Listen, I appreciate your vote of confidence, but you don't know that company as I do. A, they'd cover everything up. B, they'd drag the proceedings on so long that I would run out of money. C, *regardless* of the outcome, they'd make such a public issue of a suit that what little is left of my reputation would be shot to hell in the process. We're talking piranhas here, Bob."

"So why did you represent them?"

"Because I didn't *know*, damn it!" His shoulders slumped. "And that's the worst of it, I think. I just...didn't...know." His gaze skittered to the floor, dark brows lowered to hide his expression of deep self-dismay.

"You're human. Like the rest of us."

"Not much by way of encouragement."

Bob rose. "I wish I could do more."

"But you've done what you came to do and it's time to leave." Neil heard the bitterness in his voice, and while he detested it, he couldn't bring himself to apologize.

"I have an appointment at three." Bob's tone verged on apologetic, and Neil was quickly wary. He'd witnessed six weeks of defections, of so-called friends falling by the wayside.

Testing the waters, he extended his hand. "I haven't seen Julie in months. Let's meet for dinner sometime soon?"

"Sure thing," Bob said, smiling a little too broadly as the two shook hands.

Bob was relieved, Neil mused. The dirty work was done. And a "sure thing" for dinner was as noncommittal as Neil had feared it might be.

Moments later he was alone with an anger that approached explosive levels. Slumping into the mate of the chair Bob had just left, he pressed a finger to the crease in the center of his forehead and rubbed up and down. His head was splitting; he had to keep it together somehow. But how to remain sane when everything else was falling apart... Where was justice? Where in the hell was the justice in life?

Okay, he could understand why his working relationship with Wittnauer-Douglass would be severed after the abysmal scene six weeks ago. There had been, and was a difference of opinion. A rather drastic difference of opinion. He wouldn't have wanted to continue serving as counsel for the corporation any more than they'd wanted him to. But should he be punished this way?

His entire life was twisted. Damn it, it wasn't right!

Okay, so he'd lost Ryoden. He could have lived with that if it hadn't been for the fact that he'd also lost three other major clients in as many weeks. He was being blackballed within the corporate community. How the hell could he counter it, when the enemy was so much larger, so much more powerful?

He took several slow, measured breaths, opened his eyes and looked around the office. Ceiling-high mahogany bookshelves filled with legal tomes; an impressive collection of diplomas and brass-framed citations; a state-of-the-art telephone system linking him to his secretary and the world beyond; a credenza filled with important forms and personal papers—all worthless. What counted was in his head. But if he couldn't practice law his mind was worthless, too; it was hammering at his skull now, hammering mercilessly.

Neil Hersey had never felt so furious, so bitter—so utterly helpless—in his entire life. He knew that something had to be done, and that he was the one who was going to have to do it. For the life of him, though, he didn't know what action to take. His thoughts were mired in that fury and bitterness. He couldn't think clearly.

Muttering a dark oath, he bolted from his seat. He needed a break, a change of scenery. More than anything at the moment, he needed out.

Rounding the desk, he snatched his personal phone book from the top right-hand drawer and flipped to the Ls. Landry. Lazuk. Lee. Lesser. He set the book down, marking the place with his finger. Lesser. Victoria Lesser. Within seconds he'd punched out the number that would connect him with the stylish Park Avenue co-op high above the hustle of Manhattan.

A very proper maid answered. "Lesser residence."

"This is Neil Hersey. Is Mrs. Lesser in?"

"Please hold the phone."

Neil waited, tapping his foot impatiently. He massaged the throbbing spot on his forehead. He squeezed his eyes shut. Only when he pictured Victoria breezing toward the phone—wending her way through the most elegant of furnishings while, very likely, wearing jeans and an oversized work shirt—did he give a small smile.

Victoria Lesser was a character. Thanks to the husband she'd worshipped until his death six years earlier, she was extremely wealthy and influential. She was also a nonconformist, which was what Neil adored about her. Though never outrageous, she did what she wanted, thumbing her nose at the concept of a staid and proper fifty-two-year-old widow. She traveled. She entertained. She took up ballet dancing. She fantasized herself a painter. She was interesting and refreshing and generous to the core.

It was that generosity Neil was counting on.

"Neil Hersey...fine friend you are!" A good-natured tirade burst from the other end of the line. "Do you know how long it's been since I've heard from you? It's been months! *Months!*"

"I know, Victoria. And I'm sorry. How are you?"

"How I am is beside the point," Victoria said more softly. "The question is, how are *you*?"

Neil hadn't been sure how far word had spread, but he should have realized Victoria would have heard. The mutual friend through which they'd originally met was an executive at Wittnauer-Douglass.

"You're speaking to me," he answered cautiously, "which makes me feel better already."

"Of course I'm speaking to you. I know what happened there, Neil. I know that board of directors. That is, I know how to recognize snakes. I also know what kind of lawyer you are—I haven't forgotten what you did for my niece—and I know the bind you're in right now."

"Then you know I need to get away." He broached the topic quickly. He was in no mood, even with Victoria, to pussyfoot around. "I can't think here. I'm too angry. I need peace and quiet. And seclusion."

"Something like a remote and uninhabited island off the coast of Maine?"

Neil's mouth lifted slightly at the corners. "Something like that."

"It's yours."

"No one's there?"

"In October?" She snorted. "People nowadays are sissies. Once Labor Day's passed, you'd think going north to an island was tantamount to exploring the Arctic. It's yours, Neil, for as long as you want it."

"Two weeks should do it. If I can't come up with some solutions by then..." There wasn't much more he could say.

"You haven't called me before, and knowing you, you'll want to work this out for yourself. But if there's anything I can do, will you let me know?"

Neil found solace in her words. She had the courage that others lacked. Not only was she unswayed by smear tactics, she would root for the underdog any day. "Use of the island is more than enough," he said gratefully.

"When were you thinking of going?"

"As soon as possible. Tomorrow, I guess. But you'll have to tell me how to get there."

Victoria did so. "Once you get to Spruce Head, ask for Thomas Nye. Big fellow. Bushy red beard. He lobsters from there. I'll call ahead and alert him. He'll take you out to the island."

With brief but heartfelt thanks, plus a promise to call her when he returned, Neil hung up the phone. He spent the rest of the afternoon working with his secretary to clear his calendar for the next two weeks. It was a relatively easy feat, given the amount of work he'd recently lost. He met in turn with each of his two young associates, giving them enough direction to keep them marginally occupied during his absence.

For the first time in his memory, when he left the office his briefcase remained behind. He carried nothing more than a handful of Havana cigars.

If he was going to escape it all, he decided belligerently, he'd go all the way.

DEIRDRE JOYCE glowered at the thick white cast that sheathed her left leg from thigh to toe. It was a diversionary tactic. If she looked into the urgent faces that circled her hospital bed, she was sure she'd explode.

"It was an act of fate, Deirdre," her mother was saying. "A message. I've been trying to get it across for months now, but you've refused to listen, so someone higher up is spelling it out. Your place is in the business with your sister, not teaching aerobics."

"My teaching aerobics had nothing to do with this, Mother," Deirdre declared. "I tripped on the stairs in my own town house. I fell. I broke my leg. I don't see any message there, except that I was careless. I left a magazine where it shouldn't have been and slipped on it. It could as easily have been *Forbes* as *Runner's World.*"

"The message," Maria Joyce went on, undaunted, "is that physical fitness will only get you so far. For heaven's sake, Deirdre, you'll be sidelined for weeks. You can't teach your precious dance even if you want to. What better time is there to help Sandra out?"

Deirdre looked at her sister then. Once upon a time she'd have felt compassion for her, but that was before six months of nonstop pressure had taken its toll. "I'm sorry, Sandra. I can't."

"Why not, Dee?" Tall and dark-haired, Sandra took after their mother, while Deirdre was more fair and petite. She had been different from the start. "You have the same education I do, the same qualifications," Sandra pressed.

"I don't have the temperament. I never did."

Maria was scowling. "Temperament has nothing to do with it. You decided early on that you preferred to take the easy way out. Well, you have, and look where it's gotten you."

"Mother…" Deirdre closed her eyes and sank deeper into the pillows. Four days of confinement in a bed had left her weak, and that annoyed her. It had also left her craving a hot shower, but that was out of the question. To say that she was testy was putting it mildly.

Her voice was quiet, but there was clear conviction in her words. "We've been through this a hundred times. You and Dad may have shared the dream of a family corporation, but it's your dream, not mine. I don't want it. I'm not suited for it. It's too structured, too demanding. I gave it a try once and it was a disaster."

"Eight months," Maria argued, "years ago."

"Your mother's right, Deirdre." The deep, slightly gravelly voice belonged to Deirdre's uncle. He had been standing, silent and innocuous up to that point, at the foot of the bed. "You'd only just graduated from college, but even then you showed potential. You're a doer, like your father, but you were young and you let things overwhelm you. You left too soon. You didn't give it a fair shot."

Deirdre shook her head. "I knew myself then," she insisted, scrunching folds of the coarse white sheet between tense fingers, "and I know myself now. I'm not cut out for the business world. Having a technical aptitude for business is one thing. Maybe I do have that. But emotionally—what with board meetings, conferences, three-martini lunches, client dinners, being constantly *on*—I'd go stark raving mad!"

"You're being melodramatic," her mother scoffed.

"Right. That's the way I am, and there's no place for melodrama in Joyce Enterprises. So please," she begged, "please leave me out of it."

Sandra took a step closer. "We need you, Dee. *I* need you. Do you think I'm any more suited to heading a corporation than you are?"

"At least you want to do it."

"Whether I do or not is irrelevant. Things have been a mess since Dad died."

Since Dad died. That was the crux of it. Six months before, Allan Joyce had died in his sleep, never knowing that what he'd done so peacefully had created utter havoc.

Deirdre closed her eyes. "I think this conversation's going nowhere," she stated quietly. "The only reason things have been a mess since Dad died is that not one of you—of us—has the overall vision necessary to head a corporation. What Joyce Enterprises needs is outside help. It's as simple as that."

"We're a family-run company—" her mother began, only to stop short when Deirdre's eyes flew open, flashing.

"And we've run out of family. You can't run a business, Mother. Apparently neither can Sandra. Uncle Peter is as helpless as Uncle Max, and I'm the only one who's willing to acknowledge that the time has come for a change." She gave an exasperated sigh. "What astounds me most is that the corporation is still functioning. It's been running itself, coasting along on Dad's momentum. But without direction it's only a matter of time before it grinds to a halt. *Sell it*, Mother. And if you won't do that, hire a president and several vice presidents and—"

"We have a president and several vice presidents," Maria informed her unnecessarily. "What we lack is someone to coordinate things. You're the organizer. You're what we need. You're the one who's put together all kinds of functions."

"Charity functions, Mother. One, maybe two, a year. Benefit road races and sports days," she replied wearily. "We're not talking heavy business here."

"You're your father's daughter."

"I'm not my father."

"But still—"

"Mother, I have a wicked headache and you're not helping. Uncle Peter, will you please take Mother home?"

Maria held her ground. "Now just a minute, Deirdre. I won't be dismissed. You're being selfish. You've always put your own needs first. Don't you have any sense of responsibility toward this family?"

The guilt trip. It had been inevitable. "I'm not up to this," Deirdre moaned.

"Fine." Maria straightened. "Then we'll discuss it tomorrow. You're being discharged in the morning. We'll be here to pick you up and drive you to the house—"

"I'm not going to the house. I'm going to my place."

"With a broken leg? Don't be absurd, Deirdre. You can't climb those stairs."

"If I can't handle a flight of stairs, how can I possibly run a multimillion-dollar corporation from a seventeenth-floor office?"

"There are elevators."

"That's not the point, Mother!" Deirdre threw an arm over her eyes. She felt tired and unbelievably frustrated. It was nothing new. Just worse. "All I know," she managed stiffly, "is that I'm checking out of here tomorrow morning and going to my own town house. Where I go from there is anyone's guess, but it won't be to Joyce Enterprises."

"We'll discuss it tomorrow."

"There's nothing to discuss. It's settled."

Maria's chin gave a little twitch. It was a nervous gesture, one that appeared when she wasn't getting her way. Deirdre had caused it more times than either of them could count. "You're upset. It's understandable, given what you've been through." She patted her daughter's cheek. "Tomorrow. We'll talk tomorrow."

Deirdre said nothing. Lips set in a grim line, she watched her visitors pass one by one through the door. Alone at last, she pressed her finger hard on the call button.

Her head throbbed. Her leg throbbed. She needed aspirin.

She also needed a magic carpet to sweep her up, up and away.

This time when she glowered at her cast, there was no diversion intended. How could she have been so careless as to slip on that magazine? Why hadn't she caught herself, grabbed the banister? Why hadn't she just sat down and bumped her way to the bottom of the stairs?

But that would have been too simple. Deirdre the athlete had had to tumble head over heels. She'd had to catch her ankle in the banister, breaking her leg in three places.

Given the picture of coordination she'd projected day in day out for the past five years, it was downright embarrassing. Given the physical exertion her body was used to, her body craved, her present state was downright stifling.

It was also depressing. Her future was a huge question mark. Rather than a simple break, what she'd done to her leg had required intricate surgery to repair. She'd been trussed up in the hospital for four days. She'd be in the cast for six weeks more. She'd have to work her way through several weeks of physical therapy after that, and only *then* would she learn whether she'd be able to teach again.

As if her own problems weren't enough to bear, there was the matter of her family. . . and Joyce Enterprises. That provoked anger. Ever since her initial eight-month fiasco of a professional introduction to the company, she'd insisted that she wanted no part of it.

While he'd been alive, her father had put in repeated plugs. *Try it again, Deirdre. You'll grow to like it, Deirdre. If the business isn't for my children, who is it for, Deirdre?* After his death, her mother had picked up the gauntlet. Her sister and her uncles in turn had joined in later. And as the company had begun to fray at the edges, the pressure had increased.

Deirdre loved her own career. It was an outlet—demanding, creative and rewarding. She took pride in the fact that she was a good teacher, that she'd developed a loyal following, that her classes were packed to overflowing and that she'd become known as the queen of aerobics at the health club.

Her career had also been a convenient excuse, and now she was without.

A pair of aspirin eased the pain in her leg and, to some extent, her headache. Unfortunately, it did nothing to ease her dilemma. The prospect of leaving the hospital in the morning, and by doing so putting herself at the mercy of her family, was dismal. She could see it now—the phone calls, the drop-in visits, the ongoing and relentless campaign to draft her. Dismal. Unfair. *Unbearable.* If only there were someplace quiet, distant, secluded . . .

Sparked by a sudden determination, she grabbed the phone, dealing first with the hospital operator, then New York City information, then the hospital operator once more. At last her call went through.

A very proper maid answered. "Lesser residence."

"This is Deirdre Joyce. Is Mrs. Lesser in?"

"Please hold the phone."

Deirdre waited, tapping her finger impatiently against the plastic receiver. She shifted her weight from one bed-weary hip to the other. She squeezed her eyes shut, relieving herself of the sight of the sickroom. And she pictured Victoria, dressed no doubt in an oversized shirt and jeans, wending her way through the most elegant of surroundings to pick up the phone. Would she be coming from the music room, having just set down her cello? Or from tending African violets in her rooftop greenhouse?

Victoria was neither a musician nor a gardener, if skill was the measure. But whatever she did she loved, which was more than enough measure for Deirdre. Of all the family friends Deirdre had come to know in her twenty-nine years, Victoria Lesser was the one she most admired. Victoria was a freethinker, an individual. Rather than withering when the husband she'd loved had died, she'd blossomed and grown. She shunned parochialism and put protocol in its place. She did what she wanted, yet was always within the boundaries of good taste.

Deirdre enjoyed and respected her. It had been far too long since they'd seen each other.

"Hey, stranger," came the ebullient voice from the other end of the line, "where *have* you been?"

Deirdre gave a wan half smile. "Providence, as always, Victoria. How are you?"

"Not bad, if I do say so myself."

"What were you doing just now? I've been trying to imagine. Was it music? Gardening? Tell me. Make me smile."

"Oh-oh. Something's wrong."

For an instant Deirdre's throat grew tight. She hadn't spoken with Victoria in months, yet they could pick up a conversation as though it had been left off the day before. Despite the more than twenty years separating them, their relationship was honest.

Deirdre swallowed the knot. "What were you doing?"

"Stenciling the bathroom ceiling... Are you smiling?"

"A little."

"What's wrong, Dee?"

"I've always hated that nickname. Did you know? The only people who use it are members of my family...and you. When they do it, I feel like a child. When you do it, I feel like ... a friend."

"You are," Victoria said softly, "which is why I want you to tell me what's wrong. Are they at it again?"

Deirdre sighed and threw an arm across the mop of sandy hair on her forehead. "With a vengeance. Only this time I'm operating from a position of weakness. I broke my leg. Can you believe it? Super athlete hits the dust."

Silence.

Deirdre's voice dropped an octave. "If you're laughing at me, Victoria, so help me..."

"I'm not laughing, sweetheart. I'm not laughing."

"You're smiling. I can hear it."

"It's either that or cry. The irony of it is too much. Of all the people to break a leg, you can stand it the least . . . no pun intended. Are you going stir-crazy?"

"I can see it coming fast. It's bad enough that I can't work out. Lord only knows when—or if—I'll be able to teach again. But they're closing in on me, and they're not about to let up until I either give in and go to the office or flip out completely." She took an uneven breath. "I need to get away, Victoria. There'll be no peace here and I have to think about what I'm going to do if . . . if I can't . . ." She didn't need to finish; Victoria felt her fear.

There was a pause. "You're thinking of Maine."

"If it'd be all right with you. You've mentioned it so often, but the timing's never been right. It might be just what I need now—distant enough, quiet, undemanding."

"And there's no phone."

"You do understand."

"Uh-huh." There was another pause, then a pensive, "Mmmm. Maine might be just what you need. When were you thinking of going?"

For the first time since her fall down the stairs, Deirdre felt a glimmer of spirit. "As soon as I can." Definitely. "Tomorrow, I guess." Why not! "But you'll have to tell me how to get there."

Victoria did so, giving her route and exit numbers. "Can you get someone to drive you?"

"I'll drive myself."

"What about your broken leg?"

"It's my left one."

"Ahhh. Be grateful for small favors."

"Believe me, I am. Okay, once I get to Spruce Head, what do I do?"

"Look for Thomas Nye. Big fellow. Bushy red beard. He lobsters from there. I'll call ahead and alert him. He'll take you out to the island."

Deirdre managed a smile then. "You are a true friend, Victoria. A lifesaver."

"I hope so," Victoria replied cautiously. "Will you give me a call when you get back to let me know how things went?"

Deirdre agreed, adding heartfelt thanks before she finally hung up the phone and lay back on the bed.

Victoria, on the other hand, merely pressed the disconnect button. When the line was clear, she put through her second call in as many hours to Thomas Nye. She wore a distinct look of satisfaction when she finally returned the receiver to its cradle.

IT WAS STILL RAINING. Strike that, Neil amended sourly. It was pouring.

He scowled past his streaming windshield to the rain-spattered road ahead. The storm had followed him north, he decided. Just his luck. From Connecticut, through Massachusetts, to New Hampshire, then Maine—four-plus hours of nonstop rain. Leaden skies promised more of the same.

His windshield wipers flicked from left to right and back in double time, yet the passing landscape blurred. He hadn't minded the lack of visibility when he'd been on the superhighway—there hadn't been much to see. But he was well off the turnpike now, following Route 1 through towns such as Bath, Wiscasset and Damariscotta. He would have welcomed the diversion of an occasional "down east" sight.

But all he saw was the dappling and redappling sweep of grays and browns, in the middle of which—demanding his constant attention—was the road. The only sounds he heard were the steady beat of rain on the roof of the car and the more rhythmic, if frantic, pulse of the wipers. The world smelled wet. He was tired of sitting. And his mind . . . His mind persisted in rummaging through the baggage it had brought along on the trip.

Shortly before three in the afternoon, his mood as dark as the clouds overhead, Neil pulled his black LeBaron to a stop alongside the weathered wharf at Spruce Head. He should have been relieved that the arduous drive was over. He should have felt uplifted, filled with anticipation, eager to be nearing his destination.

What he felt was dismay. The docks were mucky. Visibility beyond the moored but wildly bobbing boats was practically nil. And the stench in the air, seeping steadily into the car, was nearly overpowering.

Distastefully he studied the large lobster tanks lined up on the wharf, then the nearby vats filled with dead fish, rotting for use as lobster bait. His own fondness for lobster meat in no way made the smell easier to take.

A gust of wind buffeted the car, driving the rain against it with renewed fury. Neil sat back in the seat and swore softly. What he needed, he decided, were a fisherman's oilskins. As far as he could see, though, not even the fishermen were venturing outside.

Unfortunately he had to venture. He had to find Thomas Nye.

Retrieving his Windbreaker from the back seat, he struggled into it. Then, on a single sucked-in breath, he opened the car door, bolted out, slammed the door behind him and raced to the nearest building.

The first door he came to opened with a groan. Three men sat inside what appeared to be a crude office, though Neil doubted he'd interrupted serious work. Each man held a mug filled with something steaming. Two of the chairs were tipped back on their hind legs; the third was being straddled backside-to.

All three men looked up at his entrance, and Neil was almost grateful for his disheveled appearance. His hair was damp and mussed; a day's worth of stubble darkened his cheeks. His Windbreaker and worn jeans were rain spattered, his running shoes mud spattered, as well. He felt right at home.

"I'm looking for Thomas Nye," he announced straightaway. Fishermen were laconic; that suited him fine. He was in no mood for polite chitchat. "Big fellow with a bushy red beard?"

One chair and one chair only hit the floor. Its occupant propped his elbows on his knees and gestured with a single hand. "Down a block . . . feust left . . . second house on y'or right."

Nodding, Neil left. Head ducked low against the torrent, he dashed back to the car and threw himself inside. Rain dripped from his Windbreaker onto the leather seats, but he paid no heed. In the short minutes since he'd arrived at Spruce Head, his focus had narrowed. Reaching Victoria's island and shutting himself inside her house to avail himself of that highly acclaimed master bedroom with its walls of glass, its huge stone fireplace and its quilt-covered king-size bed seemed all-important.

Taking a minute to decide which way was "down" the block, he started the car and set off. One left later he turned, then pulled up at the second house on the right. It was one of several in a row on the street, and he might have said it had charm had he been in a better mood. It was small, white with gray shutters and, with its paint peeling sadly, looked as aged as he felt.

Loath to waste time, he ran from the car and up the short front walk. Seeing no doorbell, he knocked loudly enough to make himself heard above the storm. Shortly the door was opened by a big fellow with a bushy red beard.

Neil sighed. "Thomas Nye."

The man nodded, held the door wide and cocked his head toward the inside of the house. Neil accepted his invitation instantly.

LESS THAN AN HOUR LATER, Deirdre pulled up at the same house. She looked in turn at the humble structure, then at the sporty black car parked in front of her. Even had she not seen the Connecticut license plate she would have bet it wasn't the car of a lobsterman.

Thomas Nye apparently had guests and the thought didn't thrill her. She wasn't exactly at her best—an assessment, she realized, that was decidedly kind.

She'd been lucky. A passerby at the wharf had given her directions, sparing her a dash from the car. Not that she could dash. Or even walk. Hobble was more like it.

But her luck had run out. She was at Thomas Nye's house and there was no way she could speak to the man without leaving the haven of her car. That meant hauling out her crutches, extricating her casted leg from the hollow to the left of the brake and maneuvering herself to a standing position. It also meant getting wet.

Well, why not! she snapped to herself. The day had been a nightmare from the start. What was a little more grief?

Tugging her hip-length Goretex parka from the back seat, she struggled into it. Then, taking a minute to work out the logistics of dealing with cast, crutches and rain, she opened the car door and set to it.

By the time she reached Thomas Nye's front door, she was gritting her teeth in frustration. What might have taken ten seconds, had she been operating on two strong legs, had taken nearly two minutes—long enough for the storm to drench her. Her hair was plastered to her head and dripping in her eyes. Her sweatpants were noticeably heavier. Her wet grip on the crutches was precarious. And her armpits ached.

Tamping down her irritation as best she could, she shifted her weight to one crutch and knocked. As the small porch overhang offered some protection from the gusting rain, she wedged herself closer to the door.

She twitched her nose. The rank odor that had hit her full force at the wharf was less pungent here, diluted by the fresh salty air and the rain.

She tugged at her collar. She was cold. Impatient, she knocked again, louder this time. Within seconds, the door was opened by a big fellow with a bushy red beard.

Deirdre sighed. "Thomas Nye."

Eyes skittering away, he nodded, held the door wide and cocked his head toward the inside of the house. She hitched her way into the narrow front hall, and at another silent gesture from the large man, into the small living room.

The first thing she saw was a low table spread with papers, charts and what looked to be bills. The second was the television set, broadcasting *Wheel of Fortune* in living color. The third was the dark, brooding figure of a man slouched in a chair in the far corner of the room.

The fourth thing she noticed, unfortunately, was that Thomas Nye had calmly settled into a seat by the table, returning to the work her knock had apparently interrupted.

She cleared her throat. "You were expecting me."

"That's right," he said. He had already lifted several papers, and didn't look up. "Want to sit?"

"Uh . . . are we . . . going?"

"Not now."

She ingested that information with as much aplomb as she could, given that the last thing she wanted was a delay. "It's the weather, I take it?" The possibility had been niggling at the back of her mind for the past hour. She'd done her best to ignore it.

The man in the corner grunted.

Thomas Nye nodded.

"Do you have any idea when we *will* be able to go?" she asked, discouraged; it seemed like forever since she'd awoken that morning. She now had to admit that making the trip on the same day as her discharge from the hospital may have been taking too much upon herself. But it was done. The best she could hope for was that the delay would be minimal.

In answer to her question, the bearded man shrugged. "As soon as it lets up."

"But it could rain for days," she returned. When a second grunt came from the man in the corner, she darted him a scowl. At the moment all she wanted was to be dry and warm beneath a heavy quilt on that king-size bed in the house on Victoria's island. Alone. With no one to stare at the sorry sight she made and no one to make her feel guilty about anything.

She willed her concentration on Nye. "I thought you went lobstering rain or no rain."

"The wind's the problem." At precisely that moment a gust howled around the house.

Deirdre shuddered. "I see." She paused. "Is there a forecast? Do you have any idea when it will let up?"

Nye shrugged. "An hour, maybe two, maybe twelve."

She leaned heavily on the crutches. An hour or two she could live with. But twelve? She doubted she could last twelve hours without that warm, dry bed and heavy quilt. And where would she be waiting out the time?

She glanced again at the man in the corner. He sat low in his chair, one leg stretched out, the other ankle crossed over his knee. His elbows were propped on the arms of the chair, his mouth pressed flush against knuckle-to-knuckle fists. His eyebrows were dark, the eyes beneath them even darker. He, too, was waiting. She could sense his frustration as clearly as she felt her own.

"Uh, Mr. Nye," she began, "I really have to get out there soon. If I don't get off this leg, I'm apt to be in trouble."

Nye was jotting something on the top of one of the papers that lay before him. He lifted his gaze to the game show and gestured with his pencil toward a faded sofa. "Please. Sit."

Deirdre watched as he resumed his work. She contemplated arguing further but sensed the futility of it. He looked calm, satisfied . . . and utterly immovable. With a grimace she plodded to the sofa. Jerking off her wet parka, she thrust it over the back of the worn cushion, coupled her crutches to one side of her and eased her way down.

When she lifted her eyes once more, she found the man in the corner staring at her. Irritated, she glared back. "Is something wrong?"

He arched a brow, lowered his fists and pursed his lips. "That's quite an outfit." It wasn't a compliment.

"Thank you," she said sweetly. "I rather like it myself." Actually, when they were dry, the roomy pink sweatpants were the most comfortable ones she owned, and comfort was a high priority, what with a cast the size of hers. Unfortunately, while dressing, she'd also been fighting with her mother, and consequently she'd pulled on the first sweatshirt that came to hand. It was teal colored, oversized and as comfortable as the pants, though it did clash slightly. And if the man had an argument with her orange leg warmers, that was his problem. The left one, stretched out and tucked into itself beyond her foot, had kept her toes warm and her cast dry. Her lone sneaker on the other foot, was pitifully wet.

So she didn't look like Jaclyn Smith advertising makeup. Deirdre didn't care. In the immediate future, she was going to be all alone on an island. No one would see her. No one would care what she wore. Practicality and comfort were the two considerations she'd made when deciding what to bring with her. The man with the dark, brooding eyes could thank his lucky stars he wouldn't have to see her beyond this day.

Muted pandemonium broke loose on the television screen as a player won a shiny red Mercedes. Looking up, Thomas grinned at the victory, but Deirdre merely lowered her head and pressed chilled fingers to the bridge of her nose. She hated game shows almost as much as she hated soap operas. On occasion when she passed through the lounge of the health club, the set would be tuned to one or the other. Invariably she'd speed on by.

Now she was speeding nowhere. That fact was even more grating than the sound of the show. Disgruntled, she shoved aside the wet strands of hair on her brow and focused on Thomas Nye.

Head tucked low once again, he was engrossed in his paperwork. He looked almost preppy, she reflected, appraising his corduroy pants, the shirt and sweater. A man of few words, and those spoken with a New York accent, he was apparently a transplant. Deirdre wondered about that. Was he antiestablishment? Antisocial? Or simply...shy? He seemed unable to meet her gaze for more than a minute, and though he was pleasant enough, he made no attempt at conversation. Nor had he introduced her to the man in the corner.

Just as well, she decided as she shifted her gaze. The man in the corner didn't appear to be anyone she'd care to meet. He was frowning toward the window now, his fist propped back against his cheek. The furrow between his brows was marked. His lips held a sullen slant. And if those signs of discontent weren't off-putting enough, the heavy shadow of a beard on his lower face gave him an even less inviting appearance.

Just then he looked her way. Their eyes met and held, until at last she turned her head. No, he wasn't anyone she'd care to meet, because he looked just as troubled as she was, and there was precious little room in her life for compassion at the moment.

At the moment, Neil Hersey was thinking similar thoughts. It had been a long time since he'd seen anyone as pathetic-looking as the woman across the room. Oh, yes, the weather had taken its toll, soaking her clothes and matting her short, brown hair in damp strands that grazed her eyelids. But it was more than that. The weather had nothing to do with the fact that she had one fat leg and an overall shapeless figure. Or that she was pale. Or that her crossness seemed to border on orneriness. He assumed Nye was shuttling her to one of the many islands in the Gulf of Maine. But he had woes enough to keep him occupied without bothering about someone else's.

His immediate woe was being landlocked. Time was passing. He wanted to be moving out. But Thomas Nye was calling the shots, a situation that only exacerbated Neil's dour mood.

He shifted restlessly and absently rubbed his hand over the rough rag wool of his sweater. Was that heartburn he felt? Maybe an incipient ulcer? He took a disgusted breath, shifted again and was about to glance at his watch, when he saw the woman do it.

"Mr. Nye?" she asked.

"Thomas," Nye answered without looking up.

"Thomas. How long will the crossing take?"

"Two hours, give or take some."

She studied her watch again, making the same disheartening calculations Neil did. "But if we're held up much longer, we won't make it before dark." It would be bad enough negotiating rugged terrain in daylight with her crutches, but at night? "That . . . could be difficult."

"Better difficult than deadly," Thomas replied gently. "As soon as the wind dies down, we'll go. We may have to wait till morning."

"Morning! But I don't have anywhere to stay," she protested.

Thomas tossed his head toward the ceiling. "I've got room."

She gave an exaggerated nod, which said *that* solved everything, when in fact it didn't. It wasn't what she wanted at all! She wanted to be on Victoria's island, comfortably settled in that spectacular master bedroom she'd heard so much about. She pictured it now—huge windows, an elegant brass bed, dust ruffles, quilt and pillows of a country-sophisticate motif. Silence. Solitude. Privacy. Oh, how she wanted that.

The awful fatigue she was fighting now she did not want. Or the ache in her leg that no amount of shifting could relieve. Or the fact that she was in a room with two strangers and she couldn't throw back her head and scream . . .

Neil had returned his attention to the window. What he saw there wasn't pleasing; the thought of spending the night in this tiny fisherman's house was even less so. *I've got room.* It was a generous enough offer, but hell, he didn't want to be here! He wanted to be on the island!

He was exhausted. The day's drive through the rain had been a tedious cap to six tedious weeks. He wanted to be alone. He wanted privacy. He wanted to stretch out on that king-size bed and know that his feet wouldn't hang over the edge. Lord only knew most everything else had gone wrong with his life lately.

"Does the boat have radar?" he asked on impulse.

"Yes."

"So we're not limited to daylight."

"No."

"Then there's still a chance of getting out today?"

"Of course there's a chance," Deirdre snapped, testy in her weariness. "There's always a chance."

Neil shot her a quelling look. "Then let's put it in terms of probability," he stated stubbornly, returning his attention to Thomas. "On a scale of one to ten, where would you put the chances of our making it out today?"

Deirdre scowled. "How can he possibly answer that?"

"He's a fisherman," Neil muttered tersely. "I'm asking for his professional estimate based on however many number of years he's worked on the sea."

"Three," Thomas said.

Deirdre's eyes were round with dismay. "On a scale of one to ten, we only get a *three*?"

Neil eyed her as though she were daft. "He's only been lobstering for three years."

"Oh." She then focused on Thomas. "What *are* the chances?

Thomas straightened a pile of papers and stood. "Right now I'd give it a two."

"A two," she wailed. "That's even worse!"

Neil glowered toward the window. Thomas stood. The Wheel of Fortune spun, gradually slowing, finally stopping on "bankrupt." The groans from the set reflected Deirdre's feelings exactly.

But she wouldn't give up. "How do you decide if we can leave?"

"The marine report."

"How often does that change?"

"Whenever the weather does."

The man in the corner snickered. Deirdre ignored him. "I mean, are there periodic updates you tune in to? How can you possibly tell, sitting here in the house, whether the wind is dying down on the water?"

Thomas was heading from the room. "I'll be back."

She looked at the man. "Where's he going?" He stared back mutely. "You're waiting to get out of here, too. Aren't you curious?"

Neil sighed. "He's getting the forecast."

"How can you tell?"

"Can't you hear the crackle of the radio?"

"I can't hear a thing over this inane show!" Awkwardly she pushed herself up, hopped to the television and turned the volume down, then hopped back. She was too tired to care if she looked like a waterlogged rabbit. Sinking into a corner of the sofa, she lifted her casted leg onto the cushions, laid her head back and closed her eyes.

Moments later Thomas returned. "Raise that to a seven. The wind's dying."

Neil and Deirdre both grew alert, but it was Neil who spoke. "Then we may make it?"

"I'll check the report in another half-hour." The lobsterman said no more, immersing himself back in his work.

The next half-hour seemed endless to Deirdre. Her mind replayed the events of the day, from her hospital discharge through the cab ride to her town house, then on to the unpleasant scene with her mother, who had been positively incensed that Deirdre would even think of leaving Providence. Deirdre would have liked to believe it was maternal concern for her health, but she knew otherwise. Her refusal to tell Maria where she was headed had resulted in even stronger reprisals, but Deirdre couldn't bear the thought that somehow her mother would get through to her on the island.

She needed this escape. She needed it badly. The way she felt, she doubted she'd get out of bed for days . . . when she finally reached the island.

Neil didn't weather the half-hour any better. Accustomed to being constantly on the move, he felt physically confined and mentally constrained. At times he thought he'd scream if something didn't happen. Everything grated—the lobsterman's nonchalance, the flicker of the television, the sight of the woman across the room, the sound of the rain. Too much of his life seemed dependent on external forces; he craved full control. Misery was private. He wanted to be alone.

At long last Thomas left the room again. Deirdre raised her head and held her breath. Neil waited tensely.

From the look on the fisherman's face when he returned, it seemed nothing had changed. Yet the first thing he did was flip off the television, then he gathered up his papers.

Aware that the man in the corner was holding himself straighter, Deirdre did the same. "Thomas?"

He said nothing, simply gestured broadly with his arms. Deirdre and Neil needed no more invitation. Within seconds, they were up and reaching for their jackets.

2

THE STORM MIGHT HAVE ABATED over the water, but Deirdre saw no letup on shore. The rain soaked her as she limped on her crutches to her car, which, at Thomas's direction, she moved to the deepest point in the driveway. Transferring her large duffle bag to the pickup was a minor ordeal, eased at the last minute by Thomas, who tossed her bag in, then returned to stowing boxes of fresh produce in the back of the truck. The other man was preoccupied, parking his own car, then loading his bag.

Gritting her teeth, she struggled into the cab of the truck. No sooner was she seated than the two men—the dark one, to her chagrin, had turned out to be every bit as large as the lobsterman—boxed her in, making the ensuing ride to the wharf damp and uncomfortable. By the time she was aboard Thomas's boat, propped on a wood bench in the enclosed pilothouse, she felt stiff and achy. Her sneaker was soggy. Her jacket and sweatpants were wet. She was chilled all over.

The nightmare continued, she mused, but at least its end was in sight. She'd be at Victoria's island, alone and in peace, by nightfall. It was this knowledge that kept her going.

The engine chugged to life and maintained an even growl as the boat left the wharf and headed seaward. Deirdre peered out the open back of the pilothouse for a time, watching Spruce Head recede and finally disappear in the mist. Burrowing deeper into her jacket, she faced forward then and determinedly focused on her destination. She pictured the island forested with pines, carpeted with moss, smelling of earth, sea and sky, kissed by the sun. She envisioned her own recovery there, the regaining of her strength, the rebirth of her spirit. And serenity. She conjured images of serenity.

Just as Neil did. Serenity...solitude... Soon, he told himself, soon. He'd wedged himself into a corner of the pilothouse, not so much to keep a distance from Nye's other passenger as to keep his body upright. It had been a long day, a long night before that. He'd grown accustomed to sleeplessness over the past weeks, but never had its effects hit him as they did now.

Though his fatigue was in large part physical, there was an emotional element as well. He was away from the office, relieved of his duties, distanced from his profession. This wasn't a vacation; it was a suspension. Brief, perhaps, but a letdown. And more than a little depressing.

A tiny voice inside accused him of running away; his abrupt departure from Hartford was sure to be seen by some as just that. Maybe he had run away. Maybe he was conceding defeat. Maybe...maybe... It was very depressing.

His pulse was steadily accelerating, as it always did when he pursued that particular line of thought. He wondered if he had high blood pressure yet. It wouldn't have surprised him, given the kind of nervous tension he'd been living with for days on end. He needed an outlet. Any outlet.

His gaze settled on the woman just down the bench. "Don't you think it's a little stupid going out in all this like that?" He jerked his chin toward the fat leg she'd painstakingly hauled up beside her on the hard bench.

Deirdre had been wondering apprehensively if the rhythmic plunge of the boat, noticeable now that they'd left the harbor behind, was going to get worse. She looked at him in disbelief. "Excuse me?"

"I said, don't you think it's a little stupid going out in all this like that?" He found perverse satisfaction in the verbatim repetition.

"That's what I thought you said, but I couldn't believe you'd be so rude." She had no patience. Not now. Not here. "Didn't your mother ever teach you manners?"

"Oh, yes. But she's not here right now, so I can say exactly what I want." Ah, the pleasure in blurting words out at will. He couldn't remember the last time he'd done it as freely. "You haven't answered my question."

"It's not worth answering." She turned her head away and looked at Thomas, who stood at the controls, holding the wheel steady. His body swayed easily with the movement of the boat. Deirdre wished she could go with the flow that way, but her own body seemed to buck the movement. She was glad she hadn't eaten recently.

In an attempt to divert her thoughts from various unpleasant possibilities, she homed in on the baseball hat Thomas had been wearing since they'd left the house. It had fared unbelievably well in the rain. "Are you a Yankees' fan, Thomas?" she called above the rumble of the motor.

Thomas didn't turn. "When they win."

"That's honest enough," she murmured under her breath, then raised her voice again. "You're originally from New York?"

"That's right."

"What part?"

"Queens."

"Do you still have family there?"

"Some."

"What were you doing before you became a lobsterman?"

A grumble came from the corner. "Leave the man alone. He's hardly encouraging conversation. Don't you think there's a message in that?"

Deirdre stared back at him. "He's a Maine fisherman. They're all tight-lipped."

"But he's not originally from Maine, which means that he *chooses* not to speak."

"I wish *you* would," she snapped. "I've never met anyone as disagreeable in my life." She swung back to the lobsterman. "How'd you get saddled with this one, Thomas? He's a peach."

Thomas didn't answer, but continued his study of the white-capped waves ahead.

Neil propped his elbow on the back of the bench, rested his cheek in his palm and closed his eyes.

Deirdre focused on a peeling panel of wood opposite her and prayed that her stomach would settle.

Time passed. The boat had the ocean to itself as it plowed steadily through the waves amid an eerie air of isolation. The smell of fish mingled with a decidedly musty odor, whether from wet clothing, wet skin or aged wood Deirdre didn't know, but it did nothing for the condition of her insides. She took to doing yoga breathing, clearing her mind, concentrating on relaxation. She wasn't terribly successful.

At length she spoke again, clearly addressing herself to Thomas. "Two hours, more or less, you said. Will it be more, in weather like this?" The rain hadn't let up and the sea was choppy, but, to her untrained eye, they were making progress.

"We're in luck. The wind's at our back."

She nodded, grateful for the small word of encouragement. Then she shifted, bending her good knee up and wrapping her arms around it.

"You look green," came an unbidden assessment from the corner.

She sighed. "Thank you."

"Are you seasick?"

"I'm fine."

"I think you're seasick."

Lips thinned, she swiveled around. "You'd like that, wouldn't you? You'd like to see me sick. What's the matter? Are *you* feeling queasy?"

"I'm a seasoned sailor."

"So am I," she lied, and turned away. Straightening her leg, she sat forward on the bench. Then, fingers clenched on its edge, she pushed herself up and hopped toward Thomas.

"How much longer?" she asked as softly as she could. She didn't want the man in the corner to hear the anxiety in her words. Unfortunately Thomas didn't hear the words at all. When he tipped his head toward her, she had to repeat herself.

"We're about halfway there," he replied eventually. On the one hand it was reassuring; halfway there was better than nothing. On the other hand, it was depressing; another full hour to endure.

"His island's near Matinicus, too?" The slight emphasis on the "his" told Thomas who she meant.

"There are several small islands in the area."

She moved closer and spoke more softly again. "Will you drop me first? I'm not sure I can take much more of this."

"I'm heading straight for Victoria's island."

She managed a wan smile and a grateful "Thank you" before maneuvering back to her seat. She avoided looking at the man in the corner. He raised her hackles. She didn't need the added aggravation, when so much of the past week had been filled with it.

Neil was brooding, thinking of the last time he'd been on a boat. A seasoned sailor? He guessed it was true. Nancy had had a boat. She loved boats. Supposedly she'd loved him, too, but that had been when he'd had the world on a string. At the first sign of trouble she'd recoiled. Granted, her brother was on the board at Wittnauer-Douglass, so she'd been in an awkward position when Neil had been summarily dismissed. Still . . . love was love . . . Or was it?

He hadn't loved Nancy. He'd known it for months, and had felt guilty every time she'd said the words. Now he had a particularly sour taste in his mouth. Her words had been empty. She hadn't loved him—she'd loved what he was. She'd been enthralled by the image of a successful corporate attorney, the affluence and prestige. With all that now in doubt, she was playing it safe. And it was just as well, he knew, a blessing in disguise, perhaps. A fair-weather lover was the last thing he needed.

He looked over at the woman on the bench. She was another can of worms entirely. Small and shapeless, unpolished, unsociable, unfeminine—quite a switch from Nancy. "What did you do to your leg?" he heard himself ask.

Deirdre raised her head. "Are you talking to me?"

He glanced around the pilothouse. "I don't see anyone else with crutches around here. Did you break it?"

"Obviously."

"Not 'obviously.' You could have had corrective surgery for a congenital defect, or for a sports injury."

A sports injury. If only. There might have been dignity in that. But falling down a flight of stairs? "I broke it," she stated curtly.

"How?"

"It doesn't matter."

"When?"

Deirdre scowled. "It doesn't *matter*."

"My Lord, and you called *me* disagreeable!"

She sighed wearily. "I'm not in the mood for talking. That's all."

"You still look green." He gave a snide grin. "Stomach churning?"

"My stomach is fine!" she snapped. "And I'm not green...just pale. It's the kind of color you catch when you've been surrounded by hospital whites for days."

"You mean you were just released?" he asked with genuine surprise.

"This morning."

"And you're off racing through the rain to get to a remote island?" Surprise gave way to sarcasm once more.

"It's only a broken leg! The rest of me is working fine." Not quite true, but an understandable fib. "And, in case you're wondering, I didn't personally request the rain. It just came!"

"You were crazy to come out. Didn't your mother try to stop you?"

She heard the ridicule in his tone and was reminded of her earlier shot at him. Hers had been offered facetiously, as had his, yet he'd unwittingly hit a raw nerve. "She certainly did, but I'm an adult, so I don't have to listen to her!" She turned her head away, but it did no good.

"You don't look like an adult. You look like a pouting child."

Her eyes shot back to him reproachfully. "Better a pouting child than a scruffy pest! Look, why don't you mind your own business? You don't know me, and I don't know you, and before long, thank goodness, this ride will be over. You don't need to take out your bad mood on me. Just stay in your corner and brood to yourself, okay?"

"But I enjoy picking on you. You rise to the occasion."

That was the problem. She was letting him get to her. The way to deal with a man of his ilk was to ignore him, which she proceeded to do. Whether it worked or not she wasn't sure, because she suspected he had freely chosen not to speak further.

But he continued to look at her. She could feel his eyes boring into her back, and she steadfastly refused to turn. The man had gall; she had to hand it to him. He wasn't spineless, as Seth had been. . . .

Seth. Sweet Seth. Parasitic Seth. He'd slipped into her world, taken advantage of her home, her job, her affections, and then turned tail and run when the family pressure had begun. Seth hadn't wanted ties. He hadn't wanted responsibility. And the last thing he'd wanted was a woman whose career demands and family responsibilities took precedence over his own needs.

The irony of it, Deirdre reflected, was that he'd had such little understanding of her. She'd never wanted Joyce Enterprises, and she'd told him so repeatedly. But he'd still felt threatened, so he'd left. In hindsight, she was better off without him.

She was drawn from her reverie when the man in the corner rose from the bench, crossed the pilothouse and positioned himself close by Thomas. He spoke in a low murmur, which, try as she might, Deirdre couldn't hear over the guttural drone of the engine.

"How much longer?" Neil asked.

Thomas glanced at one of his dials. "Half an hour."

"Where's she going?" He put a slight emphasis on the "she."

"Near Matinicus."

"Lots of islands, are there?"

"Some."

"Who gets dropped off first?"

"I'm heading straight for Victoria's island."

Neil considered that. "Look, it's okay with me if you drop her off first. She's really pretty pathetic."

Thomas's eyes remained on the sea. "I thought you didn't like her."

"I don't. She bugs the hell out of me. Then again—" he ran a hand across his aching neck "—just about anyone would bug the hell out of me right about now. She just happens to be here." He was feeling guilty, but was torn even about that. On the one hand, arguing with the woman was thoroughly satisfying. He needed to let off steam, and she was a perfect patsy. On the other hand, she was right. He'd been rude. It wasn't his normal way.

Head down, he started back toward his corner.

Deirdre, who'd been thinking just then about how badly she wanted, *needed* a bath, and what an unbelievable hassle it was going to be trying to keep her cast out of the water, stopped him mid-way. She was feeling particularly peevish. "If you think you can con Thomas into dropping you off first, don't hold your breath. He's already set a course and it happens that *my* island's up there at the top of the list."

"Shows how much *you* know," Neil mumbled under his breath. He passed her by, slid down into his corner of the bench, crossed his arms over his chest and stared straight ahead.

Deirdre passed his comment off as a simple case of sour grapes. He was an ill-humored man. Soon enough she'd be free of his company. Soon enough she'd be at the island.

"There it is," Thomas called over his shoulder a little while later. "Victoria's island."

Deirdre pushed herself to her good knee and peered through the front windshield. "I can't see a thing."

Neil, too, had risen. "No harm," he muttered.

"Do you see anything?"

"Sure. There's a dark bump out there."

"There's a world of dark bumps out there. How do you tell which one's a wave and which one's an island?"

"The island has trees."

The logic was irrefutable. "Swell," she said, sinking back into her seat. When they reached the island they'd reach the island. She'd have plenty of time to see it, time when she wouldn't be tired and uncomfortable and thoroughly out of sorts.

Neil stood by Thomas, watching the dark bump swell and rise and materialize into an honest-to-goodness land mass. It wasn't large, perhaps half a mile square, but it was surprisingly lush. Neither the rain, nor the clouds, nor the approach of dusk could disguise the deep green splendor of the pines. And the house was there, a rambling cape-style structure of weathered gray clapboard, nestling in a clearing over-looking the dock.

Deirdre was on her knee again. "That...is... beautiful," she breathed.

Neil, who was feeling rather smug at the perfection of his destination, darted her an indulgent glance. "I agree."

"For once. I was beginning to wonder if you had any taste at all."

His indulgence ended. "Oh, I've got taste, all right. Problem is that I haven't seen a thing today that even remotely appealed to it." His eyes didn't stray from her face, making his meaning clear.

It was an insult Deirdre simply couldn't let pass. "The feeling is mutual. In fact—"

"Excuse me," Thomas interrupted loudly, "I'll need everyone's help here. And it's still pouring, so we'd better work quickly." He was already cutting the engine and guiding the boat alongside the short wooden dock. "Neil, you go outside and throw the lines onto the dock, one at the bow, one at the stern. Then hop ashore and tie us up on those pilings. I'll pass supplies to you and Deirdre. Watch yourself on the dock, Deirdre. It'll be slippery."

Deirdre nodded and worked at the wet zipper of her parka, thinking what a waste it was to give a nice name like Neil to such an obnoxious man. But at least he was helping. She'd half expected him to insist on staying dry while Thomas got her set up on shore.

Neil zipped up his jacket and headed for the open pit of the boat's stern, thinking how ironic it was that a woman with as flowing a name as Deirdre should prove to be so thorny. But at least she'd agreed to help. That surprised him. Of course, Thomas hadn't exactly given her a choice.

"The line, Neil. We're here." Thomas's call ended all silent musings.

Head ducked against the rain, Neil raced to tie up the boat, bow and stern.

Biting her lip against a clumsiness foreign to her, Deirdre managed to lumber onto the dock with only a helping hand from Thomas. When she would have thanked him, he'd already turned away to begin off-loading. He handed things, first to her, then to Neil when he reached her side.

"I'll be back in a week with fresh supplies," instructed the lobsterman hurriedly. "These should be more than enough until then. Keys to the front door are in an envelope tucked in with the eggs. If you run into a problem, any kind of emergency, you can reach me on the ship-to-shore radio in the den. The directions are right beside it."

Deirdre nodded, but she was too busy concentrating on keeping her balance to answer. When her large duffel bag came over the side of the boat, she rearranged her crutches and somehow managed to hook the wide strap of the bag over her shoulder, then return the crutches to their prescribed position without falling.

Neil, busy piling boxes of supplies atop one another to keep them as dry as possible, looked up briefly when Thomas handed over his canvas cargo bag. He set it down on the dock, finished up with the supplies, put a box in one arm and the cargo bag's broad strap over his other shoulder, then turned back to thank Thomas.

The boat was already drifting away from the dock, which didn't surprise Neil. Thomas had said they'd work quickly. But there was something that did surprise him....

Deirdre, whose eyes had gone wide in alarm, cleared her throat. "Uh, Thomas?" When the boat slipped farther away, she tried again, louder this time. "Thomas?"

The engine coughed, then started.

This time it was Neil who yelled. "Nye! You've forgotten someone! Get back here!"

The boat backed around the tip of the dock, then turned seaward.

"Thomas!"

"Nye!"

"There's been a mistake!" Deirdre shrieked, shoving her dripping hair from her eyes, then pointing to Neil. "*He's* still here!"

Neil rounded on her. His face was soaked, but his eyes were hard as steel. "Of course I'm still here! This is my friend's island!"

"It's *Victoria's* island, and Victoria is *my* friend."

"*My* friend, and she didn't mention you. She said I'd have the place all to myself!"

"Which was exactly what she told me!"

They glared at each other amid the pouring rain. "Victoria who?" Neil demanded.

"Victoria Lesser. Who's your Victoria?"

"The same."

"I don't believe you. Tell me where she lives."

"Manhattan. Park Avenue."

"She is Mrs. Arthur Lesser. Tell me about Arthur."

"He's dead. She's a widow, a wonderful... wacky..."

"Conniving..."

Scowling at each other amid encroaching darkness on that windswept dock in the rain, Deirdre and Neil reached the same conclusion at once.

"We've been had," he stated, then repeated in anger, "we've been had!"

"I don't believe it," Deirdre murmured, heart pounding as she looked out to sea. "Oh, damn," she breathed. "He's going!"

Simultaneously they began to yell.

"Thomas! Come back here!"

"Nye! Turn around!"

"Thomas! Don't do this to me, Thomas! Thomas!" But Thomas was well beyond earshot and moving steadily toward the mainland.

"That creep!" Neil bellowed. "He was in on it! Victoria must have known precisely what she was doing, and he went along with it!"

Deirdre didn't remember ever being as miserable in her life. All that she'd faced at home, all that she'd escaped was nothing compared to this having been manipulated. Her frustration was almost paralyzing. She took a ragged breath and tried to think clearly. "I've come all this way, gone through hell..." She brushed the rain from her cheek and looked at Neil. "You can't stay! That's all there is to it!"

Neil, who felt rain trickling down his neck, was livid. "What do you mean, I can't stay? I don't know what brought you here, but whatever it was, I need this island more, and I have no intention of sharing it with a sharp-tongued, physically disabled . . . urchin!"

She shook her head, sure she was imagining it all. "I don't have to take this," she spat. Turning, she set her crutches before her and started along the murky dock toward the even murkier path.

Neil was beside her. "You're right. You *don't* have to take it. I'll put through a call to Thomas and get him to come back tomorrow to pick you up."

Deirdre kept her eyes on the wet boarding, then the muddy dirt path. "I have no intention of being picked up, not until I'm good and ready to leave! You can put through that call to Thomas and have him pick *you* up!"

"No way! I came here for peace and quiet, and that's exactly what I'm going to get."

"You can get peace and quiet somewhere else. You sure can't get it with me around, and I sure can't get it with you around, and I don't know how you know Victoria, but she's been a friend of my family's for years and I'm sure she'll give me the right to this place—"

"*Right* to this place? Look at you! You can barely make it to the door!"

He wasn't far off the mark. The path was wet and slippery, slowing her progress considerably. It was sheer grit that kept her going. "I'll make it," she fumed, struggling to keep her footing on the slick incline. "And once I'm inside I'm not budging."

They reached the front steps. Deirdre hobbled up, then crossed the porch to the door. Neil, who'd taken the steps by twos, was standing there, swearing. "Tucked in beside the eggs . . ." He dropped his bag under the eaves, out of the rain, set down the box he'd carried and began to rummage through it. He swore again, then turned and retraced his steps at a run.

Weakly Deirdre leaned against the damp clapboard by the door. Pressing her forehead to the wood, she welcomed its chill against her surprisingly hot temple. The rest of her felt cold and clammy. She was shaking and perilously close to tears. How could the perfect solution have gone so wrong?

And there was nothing to be done about it, at least not until tomorrow. That was the worst of it.

Then again, perhaps it wasn't so bad. Once inside the house, she intended to go straight to bed. She didn't care if it was barely seven o'clock. She was beat and cold, perhaps feverish. Neil whoever-he-was could do whatever he wanted; she was going to sleep through the night. By the time she got up tomorrow, she'd be able to think clearly.

Neil dashed up the steps, his arms laden with boxes.

"I can't believe you did that," she cried. "You've got every last one of them piled up. It's a miracle you didn't drop them on the path, and then where would I be?"

He tossed his head back, getting his hair out of his eyes and the rain out of his hair. "Be grateful I did it myself. I could have asked you to help."

She wasn't in the mood to be grateful. "The key. Can you find the key?"

He'd set the bundles down and was pushing their contents around. "I'm looking. I'm looking." Moments later he fished out an envelope, opened it, removed the key and unlocked the door.

Deirdre, who feared that if she waited much longer she'd collapse on the spot, limped immediately inside. It was dark. She fumbled for a light switch and quickly flipped it on. In one sweeping glance she took in a large living room and an open kitchen off that. To the left was a short hall, to the right a longer one. Calculating that the hall to the right would lead to bedrooms, she single-mindedly headed that way.

There were three open doors. She passed the first, then the second, correctly surmising that they were the smaller guest bedrooms. The third . . . She flipped another light switch. Ah, she'd been right. It was much as she'd imagined it—a sight for sore eyes.

Swinging inside, she slammed the door shut with her crutch and made straight for the bed. She'd no sooner reached it than her knees buckled and she sank down, letting her crutches slip unheeded to the floor. Hanging her head, she took several deep, shaky breaths. Her limbs were quivering from weakness, exhaustion or chill, or all three. She was wet, and remedying that situation had to take first priority. Though the room was cold, she simply didn't have the wherewithal to confront that problem yet.

With unsteady fingers, she worked down the zipper of her jacket, struggled out of the soggy mass and dropped it on the rag rug by the side of the bed. She began to apologize silently to Victoria for making a mess, then caught herself. After what Victoria had done, she didn't owe her a thing!

She kicked off her sodden sneaker and tugged the wet leg warmer off her cast. The plaster was intact. Gingerly she touched the part that covered her foot. Damp? Or simply cold? Certainly hard enough. So far, so good.

Bending sharply from the waist, she unzipped her duffel bag and began pushing things around in search of her pajamas. Normally the neatest of packers, she'd been in the midst of the argument with her mother that morning when she'd thrown things into the bag. She'd been angry and tired. Fortunately everything she'd brought was squishable.

She'd finally located the pajamas, when the door to the bedroom flew open and Neil burst in. He'd already taken off his jacket, shoes and socks, but his jeans were soaked up to the thigh. Tossing his cargo bag onto the foot of the bed, he planted his hands on his hips.

"What are you doing in here? This is my room."

Deirdre clutched the pajamas to her chest, more startled than anything by his sudden appearance. "I didn't see your name on the door," she argued quietly.

"This is the largest bedroom." He pointed at the bed. "That is the largest bed." He jabbed his chest with his thumb. "And I happen to be the largest person in this house."

Deirdre let her hands, pajamas and all, fall to her lap. She adopted a blank expression, which wasn't hard, given her state of emotional overload. "So?"

"So . . . I want this room."

"But it's already taken."

"Then you can untake it. The two other rooms are perfectly lovely."

"I'm glad you feel that way. Choose whichever you want."

"I want this one."

For the first time since she'd entered the room, Deirdre really looked around. Nearly two complete walls were of thick, multi-paned glass, affording a view that would no doubt be spectacular in daylight. The large, brass-framed bed stood against a third wall; out of the fourth was cut the door, flanked by low, Colonial-style matching dressers, and, at one end, the pièce de résistance; a large raised hearth. Over it all was a warm glow cast by the bedside lamp.

Deirdre looked Neil straight in the eye. "So do I."

Neil, who'd never been in quite this situation before, was thrown off balance by her quiet determination. It had been different when she'd been yelling. This was, strangely, more threatening. Deirdre whoever-she-was was a woman who knew what she wanted. Unfortunately he wanted the same thng.

"Look," he began, carefully guarding his temper, "it doesn't make sense. I need this bed for its length alone. I'm six-three to your, what, five-one, five-two? I'll be physically uncomfortable in any of the other rooms. They all have twin beds."

"I'm five-three, but that's beside the point. I have a broken leg. I need extra space, too . . . not to mention a bathtub. From what I've been told, the master bath is the only one with a tub. I can't take a shower. It'll be enough of a challenge taking a bath."

"Try," Neil snapped.

"Excuse me?"

"I said, try."

"Try what?"

"To take a bath."

"And what is that supposed to mean?"

"What do you think it means?" he asked rhetorically. "You're filthy." He hadn't been able to resist. When he'd tried logic on her, she'd turned it around to suit herself. He didn't like that, particularly when he had no intention of giving in when it came to the master bedroom.

She looked down at her mud-spattered orange leg warmer and plucked at the odious wet wool. "Of course I'm filthy. It's muddy outside, and that boat was none too clean." She raised her head, eyes flashing. "But I don't have to apologize. Look at you. You're no prize, yourself!"

Neil didn't have to look at himself to know she was right. He'd worn his oldest, most comfortable jeans and heavy sweater, and if she could see the T-shirt under the sweater.... The stormy trip had taken its toll on him, too. "I don't give a damn how I look," he growled. "That was the whole purpose in coming here. For once in my life I'm going to do what I want, when I want, where I want. And that starts with this bed."

Jaw set, Deirdre reached for her crutches. "Over my dead body," she muttered, but much of the fight had gone out of her. Whatever energy she'd summoned to trade barbs with Neil had been drained. Draping the pajamas over her shoulder, she stood. "I have to use the bathroom. It's been a long day."

Neil watched her hobble into the bathroom and close the door. Again he found himself wishing she'd yell. When she spoke quietly, wearily, he actually felt sorry for her. She looked positively exhausted.

But damn it, so was he!

Taking his cargo bag from the foot of the bed, he put it where Deirdre had been sitting. He then lifted her soaked jacket by its collar, grabbed her duffel bag by its strap and carried them down the hall to the more feminine of the two guest bedrooms.

She'd get the hint. With luck, she'd be too tired to argue. Either that, or she'd come after him once she left the bathroom, and they could fight it out some more.

He sighed, closed his eyes and rubbed that throbbing spot on his forehead. Aspirin. He needed aspirin. No. He needed a drink. No. What he really needed was food. Breakfast had been a long time ago, and lunch had been a Whopper, eaten in sixty seconds flat at a Burger King on the turnpike.

Stopping briefly in the front hall to adjust the thermostat, he returned to the kitchen, where he'd left the boxes of food piled up. Plenty for two, he mused dryly. He should have been suspicious when Thomas had continued to hand out supplies. But it had been rainy and dim, and he hadn't thought. They'd been rushing. He'd simply assumed the girl would get back on the boat when the work was done.

He'd assumed wrong. Thrusting splayed fingers through his hair, he stared at the boxes, then set about unloading them. Soon he had a can of soup on to heat and was busy making a huge ham-and-cheese sandwich.

The kitchen was comfortable. Though small, it was modern, with all the amenities he enjoyed at home. He hadn't expected any less of Victoria. At least, not when it came to facilities. What he hadn't expected was that she'd foist company on him, not when he'd specifically said that he needed to be alone.

What in the devil had possessed her to pull a prank like this? But he knew. He knew. She'd been trying to fix him up for years.

Why now, Victoria? Why now, when my life is such a goddamned mess?

The house was quiet. He wondered about that as he finished eating and cleaned up. Surely Deirdre would be finished using the bathroom. He hadn't heard a bath running. Nor had he heard the dull thud of crutches in the hall.

Not liking the possible implications of the silence, he headed for the smaller bedroom where he'd left her things.

It was empty.

Nostrils flaring, he strode down the hall to the master bedroom. *"Damn it,"* he cursed, coming to a sudden halt on the threshold. She was in bed, albeit on the opposite side from his bag. She was in his bed!

His feet slapped the wood floor as he crossed the room and came to stand on the rug by that other side of the bed. "Hey, you! What do you think you're doing?"

She was little more than a series of small lumps under the quilt. None of the lumps moved. The bedding was pulled to her forehead. Only her hair showed, mousy brown against the pillow.

"You can't sleep here! I told you that!"

He waited. She gave a tiny moan and moved what he assumed to be her good leg.

"You'll have to get up, Deirdre," he growled. "I've moved your things to the other bedroom."

"I can't," came the weak and muffled reply. "I'm . . . too tired and . . . too . . . cold."

Neil glanced helplessly at the ceiling. *Why me? Why here and now?* He lowered his gaze to the huddle of lumps. "I can't sleep in any of the other beds. We've been through this before."

"Mmm."

"Then you'll move?"

There was a long pause. He wondered if she'd fallen asleep. At last, a barely audible sound came from beneath the covers.

"No."

He swore again and shoved another agitated hand through his hair as he stared at the bundle in the bed. He could move her. He could bodily pick her up and cart her to the next bedroom.

"Don't try to move me," the bundle warned. "I'll cry rape."

"There'll be no one to hear."

"I'll call Thomas. I'll make more noise than you've ever heard."

Rape. Of all the stupid threats. Or was it? There were just the two of them in the house. It would be her word against his, and "date rape" had become the in thing. If she was cruel enough to go through with it, she could really make a scene. And a scene of that type was the last thing he needed at this point in his life.

Furious and frustrated, he wheeled around and stormed from the room. When he reached the living room, he threw himself into the nearest chair and brooded. He threw every name in the book at Victoria, threw many of the same names at Thomas, then at the woman lying in *his* bed. Unfortunately, all the name-calling in the world didn't change his immediate circumstances.

He was bone tired, yet there was enough adrenaline flowing through him to keep him awake for hours. Needing to do something, he bolted from the chair and put a match to the kindling that had so carefully been placed beneath logs in the fireplace. Within minutes, the fire was roaring. It was some comfort. Even greater comfort came from the bottle of Chivas Regal he fished from the bar. Several healthy swallows, and he was feeling better; several more, and his anger abated enough to permit him to think.

After two hours he was feeling far more mellow than he would have imagined. He wandered into the den off the shorter of the two halls and studied the directions taped beside the ship-to-shore radio. *Piece of cake.*

Unfortunately no one responded from Thomas's house.

Bastard.

Okay, Hersey. Maybe he's not back yet. After all, it was still raining, and the man was working in total darkness. No sweat. He'll be there tomorrow. And in the meantime...

Neil banked the fire, nonchalantly walked back to the master bedroom and began to strip. *Let her cry rape*, declared his muzzy brain.

Wearing nothing but his briefs—a concession that later he'd marvel he'd been sober enough to make—he turned off the light, climbed into his side of the bed and stretched out.

"Ah..." The bed was firm, the sheets fresh. He might have imagined himself in his own bed at home had it not been for the faint aroma of wood smoke that lent an outdoorsy flavor to the air. Rain beat steadily against the roof, but it, too, was pleasant, and beyond was a sweet, sweet silence.

He was on a remote island, away from the city and its hassles. Taking a deep breath, he smiled, then let his head fall sideways on the pillow and was soon sound asleep.

3

SEVERAL HOURS LATER Neil's sleep was disturbed. Brow puckering, he turned his head. The mattress shifted, but he hadn't been the one to move. He struggled to open an eye. The room was pitch-black.

When the mattress shifted again, he opened the other eye. Was it Nancy? No, Nancy never stayed the night, and he wasn't seeing Nancy anymore. Then...

It took him a minute to get his bearings, and by the time he did, a dull pounding had started at the back of his head. He rolled to his side, tucked his chin down and pulled his knees up. He'd fall back to sleep, he told himself. He'd keep his eyes closed, breathe deeply and steadily, and fall back to sleep.

A soft moan came from the far side of the bed, followed by another shift in the mattress.

Eyes flying open, Neil swore silently. Then, gritting his teeth, he moved nearer his edge of the bed and closed his eyes again.

For a time there was silence. He was nearly asleep, when another moan came. It was a closed-mouth moan, more of a grunt, and, as before, was followed by the rustle of bedding and the shimmy of the mattress.

His head throbbed. Cursing, he threw back the covers and stalked into the bathroom. The sudden light was glaring; he squinted against it as he shoved the medi-

cine chest open. Insect repellent . . . Caladryl lotion . . .
antihistamine . . . aspirin. Aspirin. He fought with the
child-proof cap for a minute and was on the verge of
breaking the bottle, when it finally opened. Shaking
three tablets into his palm, he tossed them into his
mouth, threw his head back and swallowed, then bent
over and drank directly from the tap. Hitting the light
switch with a blind palm, he returned to bed.

The aspirin had barely had time to take effect, when
Deirdre moaned and turned again. Neil bolted upright
in bed and scowled in her direction, then groped for the
lamp. Its soft glow was revealing. She was still buried
beneath the covers, but her side of the quilt was pulled
up and around every which way. Even as he watched,
she twisted, lay still for several seconds, then twisted
again.

"Deirdre!" He grasped what he calculated to be a
handful of her shoulder and shook her. "Wake up,
damn it! I can't sleep with that tossing and turning."

There was movement, independent of his shaking,
from the lumps beneath the quilt. One hand emerged,
slim fingers clutching the quilt, lowering it until a pair
of heavily shadowed and distinctly disoriented brown
eyes met his.

"Hmm?"

"You'll have to settle down," he informed her gruffly.
"It's bad enough that I have to share this bed, but I refuse to do it with a woman who can't lie still."

Her eyes had suddenly widened at the "share this
bed" part; they fell briefly to the shadowed expanse of
his naked chest, then flew back up. Slowly, slowly they
fluttered shut.

"I'm sorry," she whispered with a sincerity that momentarily took the wind from his sails.

"Were you having a nightmare?"

"No. My leg kills."

He studied the thick wedge that had to be her cast. "Is there something you're supposed to do for it? Didn't the doctor give you any instructions? Shouldn't you elevate it or something?"

Deirdre felt groggy and exceedingly uncomfortable. "They kept it hitched up in the hospital—to minimize swelling—but I thought that was over."

"Great." Neil threw off the covers and headed for the door. "I'm stuck here with a dimwit whose leg may swell to twice its normal size." His voice was loud enough to carry clearly back to her from the hall. "And if that happens your circulation may be cut off by the cast, and if *that* happens, gangrene may set in. Terrific." He stomped back into the master bedroom, carrying two pillows under each arm, went straight to her side of the bed and unceremoniously hauled back the quilt.

"What are you doing?" she cried, blinking in confusion.

"Elevating your leg." He had two of the pillows on the bed and was trying to sort out the legs of her pajamas. "There's so much damned material here . . . Can you move your good leg? There, I've got it." With surprising gentleness, he raised her casted leg just enough to slip the pillows underneath.

"Gangrene won't set in," she argued meekly. "You don't know what you're talking about."

"At least I know enough to prop up your leg." With a flick of his wrist, he tossed the quilt back over her as he rounded the bed to reach his side. "That feels better, doesn't it?"

"It feels the same."

"Give it a minute or two. It'll feel better." He turned off the light and climbed back into bed, dropped his head to the pillow and massaged his temple. Seconds later he was up again, this time heading back to the bathroom. When he returned, he carried a glass of water and two pills. "Can you sit up?"

"Why?"

"Because I think you should take these."

The only light in the room was the sliver that spilled from the bathroom. The dimness made Deirdre feel at a marked disadvantage to the man who loomed above her. "What are they?"

"Aspirin."

He was so large...shadowed...ominous. He wasn't wearing much. What did he intend? "I don't take pills."

"These are harmless."

"If they're harmless, why should I bother to take them?"

"Because they may just help the ache in your leg, and if that happens you'll lie quietly, and then maybe I'll be able to sleep."

"You can always try another bedroom."

"No way, but that's beside the point. Right now we're discussing your taking two innocent aspirin."

"How do I know they're innocent? How do I know they're aspirin at all? I don't know you. Why should I trust anything you give me?"

Amazed that Deirdre whoever-she-was could be as perverse in the middle of the night as she was during the day, he gave an exasperated sigh. "Because, A, I took these pills from a bottle marked Aspirin, which I found in Victoria's medicine chest. B, I took three of them myself a little while ago, and I'm not up, down or dead yet. And C, I'm Victoria's friend, and that's about as good a character reference as you're going to get." He sucked in a breath. "Besides, it works both ways, you know."

"What does?"

"Character references. I have to trust that you're clean—"

"What do you mean, clean?"

"That you don't have any perversions, or addictions, or contagious diseases . . ."

"Of course I don't!"

"How can I be sure?"

"Because I'm Victoria's friend—"

"And Victoria knowingly stuck us together, so we have to trust that neither of us is an unsavory character, because we both do trust Victoria. At least I do. Or did." He threw his clenched fist in the air. "I don't believe I'm standing here arguing. Do you, or do you not, want the damn aspirin?" His fist dropped and opened, cradling the tablets.

"I want them."

Neil let out an exaggerated breath. "Then we're back where we started. Can you sit up?" He spoke the last very slowly, as though she might not understand him otherwise.

Deirdre was beyond taking offense. "If I can't, I have no business doing what I do," she muttered to herself, and began to elbow her way up. With her leg elevated, the maneuvering was difficult. Still, she was supposedly agile, an athlete, an expert at bending and twisting . . .

Neil didn't wait to watch her fall. He came down on a knee on the bed, curved his arm beneath her back and propped her up. "The pills are in my right hand. Can you reach them?"

His right hand was by her waist; his left held the glass. She took the tablets, pressed them into her mouth and washed them down with the water he offered.

Neither of them spoke.

Neil lowered her to the sheets, removed his knee from the bed and walked back to the bathroom. Quietly he set the glass by the sink, switched off the light and returned to bed.

Deirdre lay silent, unmoving, strangely peaceful. Her leg felt better; her entire body felt better. She closed her eyes, took a long, slow breath and drifted into a deep, healing sleep.

When she awoke it was daylight—overcast still, raining still, but daylight nonetheless. She lay quietly, gradually assimilating where she was and what she was doing there. As the facts crystallized, she realized that she wasn't alone in the bed. From its far side came a quiet breathing; she turned her head slowly, saw the large quilt-covered shape of Victoria's other friend, turned her head back. Then the crux of her dilemma hit her.

She'd fled Rhode Island, driven for hours in the pouring rain, been drenched, mud spattered, nearly seasick—all to be alone. But she wasn't. She was marooned on an island, some twenty miles from shore, with a grump of a man. Now what was she going to do?

Neil was asking himself the same question. He lay on his side with his eyes wide open, listening to the sounds of Deirdre's breathing, growing more annoyed by the minute. He did believe what he'd said the night before. If she was Victoria's friend—and she knew a convincing amount about Victoria—she couldn't be all bad. Still, she was disagreeable, and he wanted to be alone.

Pushing back the quilt, he swung his legs to the floor, then paused to give his head a chance to adjust to the shift in position. His head ached, though he was as ready to blame it on Deirdre as on the amount of Scotch he'd drunk the evening before.

"Don't you have something decent to wear?" came a perturbed voice from beneath the quilt.

His head shot around. Mistake. He put the heels of his hands on his temples and inch by inch faced forward. "There's nothing indecent about my skin," he gritted.

"Don't you have pajamas?"

"Like yours?"

"What's wrong with mine? They're perfectly good pajamas."

"They're men's pajamas." Even as he said it his arm tingled. It was his right arm, the one he'd used to prop her up. Sure, she'd been wearing men's pajamas, but beneath all the fabric was a slender back, a slim waist and the faintest curve of a hip.

"They're comfortable, and warm."

"I don't need warmth," he growled roughly.

"It's freezing in here. Isn't there any heat?"

"I like my bedroom cold."

"Great." It was an argument to be continued later. For the moment, there was something more pressing.

Vividly she recalled the sight of his chest, the corded muscles, the dark swirls of hair. "It might have been considerate of you to put *something* on when you decided to crawl into bed with me."

"Be grateful for the consideration I did make. I usually sleep in the buff."

She clenched a fistful of quilt by her cheek. "So macho."

"What's the matter?" he shot back. "Can't handle it?"

"There's nothing to handle. Macho has never turned me on."

"Not enough woman for it?"

The low blow hit hard, causing her to lash out in self-defense. "Too much of a woman. I hate to disillusion you, but machismo is pretty shallow."

"Ah, the expert."

"No. Simply a modern woman."

Muttering a pithy curse, Neil pushed himself from bed. "Save it for Thomas when he comes back for you later. Right now, I need a shower."

She started to look up, but caught herself. "I need a bath."

"You had your chance last night and you blew it. Now it's my turn."

"Use one of the other bathrooms. They've got showers."

"I like this one."

"But it's the only one with a tub!"

"You can have it as soon as I'm done."

"What happened to chivalry?"

"Talk of chivalry from a modern woman?" he chided, and soundly closed the bathroom door behind him.

Deirdre did look up then. He'd had the last word...so he thought. Rolling to her side, she grabbed her crutches from the floor and hobbled from the bedroom. Off the short hall on the other side of the living room was a den, and in the den was the ship-to-shore radio.

She checked her watch. Ten-forty-five. *Ten-forty-five*? She couldn't believe she'd slept round the clock and then some! But she'd needed it. She'd been exhausted. And she'd slept soundly once she'd been settled with her leg propped up and aspirin dispersing through her system.

Ten-forty-five. Had she missed Thomas? Would he be home or out on the boat? It was rainy, true, but windy?

She studied the directions beside the radio and, after several unsuccessful attempts, managed to put through the call. A young man responded, clearly not the lobsterman.

"It's urgent that I reach Thomas," she said.

"Is there an emergency?" the young man asked.

"Not exactly an emergency in the critical sense of the word, but—"

"Are you well?"

"Yes, I'm well—"

"And Mr. Hersey?"

Hersey. "Neil? He's well, too, but it really is important that I speak with Thomas."

"I'll have him call you as soon as he can."

She tightened her fingers on the coiled cord of the speaker. "When do you think that will be?"

"I don't know."

"Is he on the boat?"

"He's in Augusta on business."

"Oh. Is he due back today?"

"I believe so."

Frustration. She sighed. "Well, please give him the message."

After the young man assured her he would, Deirdre replaced the speaker and turned off the set. In Augusta on business. She wondered. Thomas would know precisely why she was calling; he'd known precisely what he was doing yesterday when he left both of his unsuspecting passengers on Victoria's island together.

She thought back to the things he'd said. He'd been smooth. She had to hand it to him. He'd been general enough, vague enough. He'd never lied, simply given clever, well-worded answers to her questions.

She wasn't at all sure she could trust him to call back.

Scowling, she turned at the sound of footsteps in the hall. So Neil had finished his shower, had he? And what was he planning to do now? She listened. The footsteps receded, replaced by the sound of the refrigerator door opening, then closing. He was in the kitchen. Good. Now she'd take her bath, and she'd take her sweet time about it.

In truth, she couldn't have rushed if she'd wanted to. Maneuvering herself into the tub was every bit the hassle she'd expected. Particularly awkward—and annoying—was the fact that the tub was flush against one wall, and in order to drape her casted leg over its lip she had to put her back to the faucets. Her decision to climb in before she ran the water resulted in a considerable amount of contortion, not to mention the fact that when she tried to lie back, the spigot pressed into her head. She finally managed to wedge herself into a corner, which meant that she was lying almost diagonally in the tub.

It was better than nothing, or so she told herself when she gave up the idea of relaxing to concentrate on getting clean. That, too, was a trial. With both hands occupied soaping and scrubbing, she slid perilously low in the water. Just as well, she reasoned. Her hair needed washing as badly, if not more than the rest of her. How long had it been since she'd had a proper shampoo? A week?

"Yuk."

Tipping her head back, she immersed her hair, doused it with shampoo and scrubbed. Unfortunately she'd used too much shampoo. No amount of dipping her head in the water removed it completely, and by then the water was dirty. She was thoroughly disgusted. In the end she drained the tub, turned on fresh warm water, sharply arched her back to put her head in the stream and hoped for the best.

By the time she'd awkwardly made her way out of the tub, she was tense all over. So much for a refreshing bath, she mused. But at least she was clean. There was some satisfaction in that. There was also satisfaction in rubbing moisturizing lotion over her body, a daily ritual that had been temporarily abandoned during her stay in the hospital. The scent of it was faint but familiar. When she closed her eyes she could imagine that she was back home, in one piece, looking forward to the day.

She couldn't keep her eyes closed forever, though, and when she opened them, the truth hit. She was neither home, nor in one piece, nor looking forward to the day. Rather, she was in self-imposed exile on Victoria's island. Her left leg was in a heavy cast, her face was decidedly pale and she was pathetically weak. And she was not looking forward to the day, because *he* was here.

Angrily she tugged on her underwear, then the mint green warm-up suit she'd brought. It was loose, oversized and stylish, and the top matched the bottom. He couldn't complain about her clothes today.

Propping herself on the toilet seat, she worked a pair of white wool leg warmers over her cast, then her good leg, put a single white crew sock on the good foot, then a single white sneaker. She towel-dried her hair with as much energy as she could muster, then, leaning against the sink, brushed it until it shone.

She studied her face. A lost cause. Squeaky clean, but a lost cause nonetheless. It was pale, bland, childlike. She'd always looked younger than her years. When she'd been in her late teens and early twenties, she'd hated it. Now, with women her age doing their best to look younger, she had her moments of self-appreciation. This wasn't one of them. She looked awful.

A pouting child? Perhaps, but only because of *him*. With a deep breath, she turned from the mirror and began to neaten the bathroom. *Him.* What an unpleasant man, an unpleasant situation. And a remedy? There was none, until she reached Thomas, until she convinced him that, for her sanity alone, Neil Hersey should be removed from the island.

A few minutes later, she entered the kitchen to find the remnants of bacon smoke in the air, two dirty pans on the stove, the counter littered with open cartons of juice and milk, a bowl of eggs, a tub of margarine, an open package of English muffins and miscellaneous crumbs. Neil Hersey was nonchalantly finishing his breakfast.

"You're quite a cook," she remarked wryly. "Does your skill extend to cleaning up after yourself, or were you expecting the maid to come in and do it?"

Neil set down his fork, rocked back in his chair and studied her. "So that's why Victoria sent you along. I knew there had to be a reason."

Deirdre snickered. "If you think I'm going to touch this disaster area, you're crazy. You made the mess, you clean it up."

"And if I don't?"

"Then you'll have spoiled juice and milk, stale muffins and dirty dishes to use next time." She stared at the greasy pans. "What did you make, anyway?"

"Bacon and eggs. Sound tempting?"

Her mouth was watering. "It might if you didn't use so much fat. I'd think that at your age you'd be concerned about that, not to mention the cholesterol in however many eggs you ate."

"Four. I was hungry. Aren't you? You didn't have supper."

"I had other things on my mind last night." She sent him a look of mock apology and spoke in her sweetest tone. "I'm sorry. Were you waiting for me to join you for dinner?"

His lips twisted. "Not quite. I had better company than you could ever be."

"A bottle of Scotch?" At his raised brows, she elaborated. "It's sitting right there in the living room with a half-empty glass beside it. Now that was brilliant. Do you always drown your sorrows in booze?"

The front legs of his chair hit the floor with a thud. "I don't drink," he stated baldly.

"Then we must have a little gremlin here who just happened to get into the liquor cabinet."

Faint color rose on Neil's neck. "I had a couple of drinks last night, but I'm not a drinker." He scowled. "And what's it to you? I came here to do what I want, and if that means getting drunk every night, amen."

He was being defensive, and Deirdre found she liked that. Not just because she was momentarily on top. There was something else, something related to that hint of a blush on his neck. "You know, you're really not all that bad-looking." Her gaze fell to take in his large, maroon-and-white rugby shirt and slimmer fitting jeans. "Aside from a receding hairline and all that crap you've got on your face—"

Neil reacted instantly. His eyes narrowed and his jaw grew tight. "My hairline is not receding. It's the same one I've had for years, only I don't choose to hide it like some men do. And as for 'all that crap' on my face, they're whiskers, in case you didn't know."

"You could have shaved."

"Why should I?"

"Because I'm here, for one thing."

"Through no choice of mine. This is my vacation you're intruding on, and the way I see it, you don't have any say as to what I do or how I look. Got that?"

Deirdre stared mutely back at him.

"Got that?" he repeated.

"I'm not hard of hearing," she said quietly.

He rolled his eyes. "Thank goodness for that, at least."

"But you've got it wrong. You're the one who's intruding on my time here, and I'll thank you to make yourself as invisible as possible until Thomas comes to pick you up."

Neil stood then, drew himself up and slowly approached her. "Make myself invisible, huh? Just how do you suggest I do that?"

He came closer and closer. Even barefoot he towered over her. Deirdre tipped back her head, stubbornly maintaining eye contact, refusing to be cowed. "You can clean up the kitchen when you're done, for one thing."

"I would have done that, anyway... when I was done."

"For another, you can busy yourself exploring the island."

"In the rain?"

"For a third, you can take yourself and your things to one of the other bedrooms."

His voice suddenly softened. "You didn't like my taking care of you last night?"

His question hung in the air. It wasn't that the words were shocking, or even particularly suggestive, but something about his nearness made Deirdre's breath catch in her throat. Yes, he was large, but that wasn't it. Yes, he looked roguish, but that wasn't it, either. He looked... he looked... warm... gentle... deep?

Neil, too, was momentarily stunned. When he'd come up so close, he hadn't quite expected—what? That she should smell so fresh, so feminine? That the faint, nearly transparent smattering of freckles on the bridge of her nose should intrigue him? That she should have dusty brown eyes, the eyes of a woman?

Swallowing once, he stepped back and tore his gaze from hers. It landed on the littered counter. With but a moment's pause, he began to close containers and return them to the refrigerator. "How does your leg feel?"

"Okay," Deirdre answered cautiously.

"Any worse than yesterday?"

"No."

He nodded and continued with his work.

Deirdre took a breath, surprised to find herself slightly shaky. "I, uh, I tried to call Thomas. He wasn't in."

"I know."

So he'd tried, too. She should have figured as much. Hobbling on her crutches to the stool by the counter peninsula, she propped herself on its edge. "We have to find a solution."

"Right."

"Any thoughts on it?"

His head was in the refrigerator, but his words carried clearly. "You know them."

She certainly did. "Then we're stalemated."

"Looks that way."

"I guess the only thing to do is to dump the problem in Victoria's lap. She caused it. Let her find a solution."

The refrigerator door swung shut. Neil straightened and thrust a hand on his hip. "That's great. But if we can't reach Thomas, how in the hell are we going to reach Victoria?"

"We'll just have to keep trying."

"And in the meantime?"

She grinned. "We'll just have to keep fighting."

Neil stared at her. It was the first time he'd seen her crack a smile. Her teeth were small, white and even; her lips were soft, generous. "You like fighting."

"I never have before, but, yeah, I kinda like it." She tilted her head to the side, tipped her chin up in defiance. "It feels good."

"You are strange, lady," he muttered as he transferred the dirty pans to the sink with more force than necessary. "Strange."

"Any more so than you?"

"There's nothing strange about me."

"Are you kidding? I haven't been arguing in a vacuum, you know. You even admitted that you enjoy picking on me. I dare you to tell me how that's any different from my saying I like fighting."

He sent a leisurely stream of liquid soap onto a sponge. "Give me a break, will you?"

"Give *me* a break, and hurry up, will you? I'm waiting to use the kitchen, or have you forgotten? It's been twenty-four hours since I've eaten—"

"And whose fault is that? If you'd stayed home where you belonged, you wouldn't have missed any meals."

"Maybe not, but if I'd stayed home, I'd have gone crazy!"

Neil stared at her over his shoulder; Deirdre stared back. The question was there; he was on the verge of asking it. She dared him to, knowing she'd take pleasure in refusing him.

In the end he didn't ask. He wasn't sure he wanted to know what she'd left that was so awful. He wasn't sure he wanted to think of someone else's problems. He wasn't sure he wanted to feel sympathy for this strange woman-child.

Perversely disappointed, Deirdre levered herself from the stool, fit her crutches under her arms and swung into the living room. Though it was the largest room in the house, it had a feel of coziness. Pine, dark stained and rich, dominated the decor—wall paneling; rafters and pillars; a large, low hub of a coffee table, and the surrounding, sturdy frames of a cushioned sofa and chairs. The center of one entire wall was bricked into a huge fireplace. Deirdre thought she'd very much like to see the fire lit.

Propping her hip against the side of one of the chairs, she gave the room a sweeping overview. No doubt about it, she mused sadly. The room, the house, the island—all had high potential for romance. Miles from nowhere... an isolated, insulated retreat... fire crackling mingled with the steady patter of rain. At the right time, with the right man, it would be wonderful. She could understand why so many of Victoria's friends had raved about the place.

"It's all yours," Neil said. Momentarily confused, Deirdre frowned at him. "The kitchen. I thought you were dying of hunger."

The kitchen. "I am."

"Then it's yours."

"Thank you."

He stepped back, allowing more than ample room for her to pass. "There's hot coffee in the pot. Help your-self."

"Thank you."

Just as she was moving by, he leaned forward. "I make it thick. Any objections?"

She paused, head down. "What do you think?"

"I think yes."

"You're right. I like mine thin."

"Add water."

"It tastes vile that way."

"Then make a fresh pot."

"I will." She looked up at him. His face was inches away. Dangerous. "If you don't mind . . ."

Taking the hint, he straightened. She swung past him and entered the kitchen, where she set about preparing a meal for the first time in a week.

It was a challenge. She began to remove things from the refrigerator, only to find that she couldn't possibly handle her crutches and much else at the same time. So she stood at the open refrigerator, balancing herself against the door, taking out one item, then another, lining each up on the counter. When she'd removed what she needed, she balanced herself against the counter and, one by one, moved each item in line toward the stove. A crutch fell. Painstakingly she worked her way down to pick it up, only to have it fall again when she raised her arm a second time.

For a woman who'd always prided herself on economy of movement, such a production was frustrating. She finally gave up on the crutches entirely, resorting alternately to leaning against counters and hopping. Each step of the preparation was an ordeal, made all the worse when she thought of how quickly and effortlessly she'd normally do it. By the time she'd finally poured the makings of a cheese omelet into the pan, she was close to tears.

Lounging comfortably on the sofa in the living room, Neil listened to her struggles. It served her right, he mused smugly. She should have stayed at home—wherever that was. Where was it? He wondered what would have driven her crazy had she not left, then he chided himself for wondering when he had worries aplenty of his own.

He thought of those worries and his mood darkened. Nothing had changed with his coming here; the situation would remain the same in Hartford regardless of how long he stayed away. He had to think. He had to analyze his career, his accomplishments and aspirations. He had to decide on a positive course of action.

So far he was without a clue.

The sound of shattering glass brought his head up. "What the hell..." He was on his feet and into the kitchen within seconds.

Deirdre was gripping the stove with one hand, her forehead with another. She was staring at the glass that lay broken in a puddle of orange juice on the floor. "What in the devil's the matter with you?" he yelled. "Can't you manage the simplest little thing?"

Tear-filled eyes flew to his. "No, I can't! And I'm not terribly thrilled about it!" Angrily she grabbed the sponge from the sink and knelt on her good knee.

"Let me do that," Neil growled, but she had a hand up, warding him off.

"No! I'll do it myself!" Piece by piece, she began gathering up the shards of broken glass.

He straightened slowly. She was stubborn. And independent. And slightly dumb. With her cast hooked precariously to the side, her balance was iffy at best. He imagined her losing it, falling forward, catching herself on a palm, which in turn would catch its share of glass slivers.

Grabbing several pieces of paper towel, he knelt, pushed her hands aside and set to work cleaning the mess. "There's no need to cry over spilled milk," he said gently.

"It's spilled orange juice, and I'm not crying." Using that same good leg, she raised herself. Her thigh muscles labored, and she cringed to think how out of shape she'd become in a mere week. "You don't have to do that."

"If I don't, you're apt to do even worse damage."

"I can take care of myself!" she vowed, then turned to the stove. The omelet was burning. "Damn!" Snatching up a spatula, she quickly folded the egg mixture in half and turned off the heat. "A crusty omelet. Just what I need!" Balling her hands against the edge of the stove, she threw her head back. "Damn it to hell. Why me?"

Neil dumped the sodden paper towels in the wastebasket and reached for fresh ones. "Swearing won't help."

"Wanna bet!" Her eyes flashed as she glared at him. "It makes me feel better, and since that's the case, I'll do it as much as I damn well please!"

He looked up from his mopping. "My, my, aren't we in a mood."

"Yes, we are, and you're not doing anything to help it."

"I'm cleaning up."

"You're making me feel like a helpless cripple. I told you I'd do it. I'm not totally incapacitated, damn it!"

He sighed. "Didn't anyone ever tell you that a lady shouldn't swear?"

Her lips twisted. "Oh-ho, yes. My mother, my father, my sister, my uncles—for years I've had to listen to complaints." She launched into a whiny mimic and tipped her head from one side to the other. "'Don't say that, Deirdre,' or 'Don't do that Deirdre,' or 'Deirdre, smile and be pleasant,' or 'Behave like a lady, Deirdre.'" Her voice returned to its normal pitch, but it held anger. "Well, if what I do isn't ladylike, that's tough!" She took a quick breath and added as an afterthought, "And if I want to swear, I'll do it!"

With that, she hopped to the counter stool and plopped down on it with her back to Neil.

Silently he finished cleaning the floor. He poured a fresh glass of juice, toasted the bread she'd taken out, lightly spread it with jam and set the glass and plate before her. "Do you want the eggs?" he asked softly.

She shook her head and sat for several minutes before slowly lifting one of the slices of toast and munching on it.

Neil, who was leaning against the counter with his ankles crossed and his arms folded over his chest, studied her defeated form. "Do you live with your family?"

She carefully chewed what was in her mouth, then swallowed. "Thank God, no."

"But you live nearby."

"A giant mistake. I should have moved away years ago. Even California sounds too close. Alaska might be better—northern Alaska."

"That bad, huh?"

"That bad." She took a long, slow drink of juice, concentrating on the cooling effect it had on her raspy throat. Maybe she was coming down with a cold. It wouldn't surprise her, given the soaking she'd taken the day before. Then again, maybe she'd picked up something at the hospital. That was more likely. Hospitals were chock-full of germs, and it would be just her luck to pick one up. Just her luck. "Why are you being so nice?"

"Maybe I'm a nice guy at heart."

She couldn't bear the thought of that, not when she was in such a foul mood herself. "You're an ill-tempered, scruffy-faced man."

Pushing himself from the counter, he muttered, "If you say so," and returned to the living room, where he sat staring sullenly at the cold hearth while Deirdre finished the small breakfast he'd made for her. He heard her cleaning up, noted the absence of both audible mishaps and swearing and found himself speculating on the kind of person she was at heart. He knew about himself. He wasn't really ill-tempered, only a victim of circumstance. Was she the same?

He wondered how old she was.

By the time Deirdre finished in the kitchen, she was feeling a little better. Her body had responded to nourishment; despite her sulky refusal, she'd even eaten part of the omelet. It was more overcooked than burned and was barely lukewarm by the time she got to it, but it was protein. Her voice of reason said she needed that.

Turning toward the living room, she saw Neil sprawled in the chair. She didn't like him. More accurately, she didn't want him here. He was a witness to her clumsiness. That, on top of everything else, embarrassed her.

In the back of her mind was the niggling suspicion that at heart he might well be a nice guy. He'd helped her the night before. He'd helped her this morning. Still, he had his own problems; when they filled his mind, he was as moody, as curt, as churlish as she was. Was he as much of a misfit as she sometimes felt?

She wondered what he did for a living.

With a firm grip on her crutches, she made her way into the living room, going first to the picture window, then retreating until she was propped against the sofa back. From this vantage point she could look at the world beyond the house. The island was gray and wet; its verdancy made a valiant attempt at livening the scene, but failed.

"Lousy day," Neil remarked.

"Mmm."

"Any plans?"

"Actually," she said with a grand intake of breath, "I was thinking of getting dressed and going to the theater."

He shook his head. "The show's sold out, standing room only. You'd never make it, one-legged."

"Thanks."

"Don't feel bad. The show isn't worth seeing."

"Not much is nowadays," she answered. If she was going to be sour, she mused, she might as well do it right. By nature she was an optimist, choosing to gloss over the negatives in life. But all along she'd known the negatives were there. For a change, she wanted to look at them and complain. It seemed to her she'd earned the right.

"I can't remember the last time I saw a good show, or, for that matter, a movie," she began with spirited venom. "Most of them stink. The stories are either so pat and contrived that you're bored to tears, or so bi-

zarre that you can't figure out what's happening. The
settings are phony, the music is blah and the acting is
pathetic. Or maybe it's the casting that's pathetic. I
mean, Travolta was wonderful in *Saturday Night Fever*. He took Barbarino one step further—just suave
enough, just sweet enough, just sensitive enough and
born to dance. But a newspaper reporter in *Perfect*? Oh,
please. The one scene that might have been good was
shot in the exercise class, but the camera lingered so
long on Travolta's pelvis it was disgusting!"

Neil was staring at her, one finger resting against his
lips. "Uh, I'm not really an expert on Travolta's pelvis,
disgusting or otherwise."

"Have *you* seen anything good lately?"

"In the way of a pelvis?"

"In the way of a movie."

"I don't have time to go to the movies."

"Neither do I, but if there's something I want to see—
a movie, an art exhibit, a concert—I make time. You
never do that?"

"For basketball I do."

She wondered if he himself had ever played. He had
both the height and the build. "What team?"

"The Celtics."

"You're from Boston?"

"No. But I got hooked when I went to school there.
Now I just drive up whenever I can get my hands on
tickets. I also make time for lectures."

"What kind of lectures?"

"Current affairs-type talks. You know, by politi-
cians or business superstars—Kissinger, Iacocca."

Her eyes narrowed. "I'll bet you'd go to hear John
Dean speak."

Neil shrugged. "I haven't. But I might. He was intimately involved in a fascinating period of our history."

"He was a criminal! He spent time in prison!"

"He paid the price."

"He named his price—books, a TV miniseries, the lecture circuit—doesn't it gall you to think that crime can be so profitable?"

Moments before, the conversation had been purely incidental; suddenly it hit home. "Yes," he said stiffly, "it galls me."

"Yet you'd pay money to go hear someone talk about his experiences on the wrong side of the law?"

Yes, he would have, and he'd have rationalized it by saying that the speaker was providing a greater service by telling all. Now, though, he thought of his experience at Wittnauer-Douglass and felt a rising anger. "You talk too much," he snapped.

Deirdre was momentarily taken aback. She'd expected him to argue, either for her or against her. But he was cutting the debate short. "What did I say?"

"Nothing," he mumbled, sitting farther back in his seat. "Nothing important."

"Mmm. As soon as the little lady hits a raw nerve, you put her down as 'nothing important.'"

"Not 'nothing important,' as in you. As in what you said."

"I don't see much difference. That's really macho of you. Macho, as in coward."

Neil surged from his chair and glared at her. "Ah, hell, give me a little peace, will ya? All I wanted to do was to sit here quietly, minding my own business."

"You were the one who talked first."

"That's right. I was trying to be civil."

"Obviously it didn't work."

"It would have if you hadn't been spoiling for a fight."

"Me spoiling for a fight? We were having a simple discussion about the ethics involved in giving financial support to convicted political criminals, when you went off the handle. I asked you a simple question. All you had to do was to give me a simple answer."

"But I don't have the answer!" he bellowed. A vein throbbed at his temple. "I don't have answers for lots of things lately, and it's driving me out of my mind!"

Lips pressed tightly together, he stared at her, then whirled around and stormed off toward the den.

4

WITH NEIL'S EXIT, the room became suddenly quiet. Deirdre listened, knowing that he'd be trying to reach Thomas again. She prayed he'd get through, for his sake as well as hers. She and Neil were like oil and water; they didn't mix well.

Taking advantage of the fact that she had the living room to herself, she stretched out on the sofa, closed her eyes and pretended she was alone in the house. It was quiet, so quiet. Neither the gentle patter of rain nor the soft hum of heat blowing through the vents disturbed the peaceful aura. She imagined she'd made breakfast without a problem in the world, and that the day before she'd transferred everything from Thomas's boat without a hitch. In her dream world she hadn't needed help, because her broken leg was good as new.

But that was her dream world. In reality, she had needed help, and Neil Hersey had been there. She wondered what it would be like if he were a more even-tempered sort. He was good-looking; she gave that to him, albeit begrudgingly. He was strong; she recalled the arm that had supported her when he'd brought her aspirin, remembered the broad chest she'd leaned against. He was independent and capable, cooking for himself, cleaning up both his mess and hers without a fuss.

He had potential, all right. He also had his dark moments. At those times, given her own mood swings, she wanted to be as far from him as possible.

As she lay thinking, wondering, imagining, her eyelids slowly lowered, and without intending to, she dozed off. A full hour later she awoke with a start. She'd been dreaming. Of Neil. A lovely dream. An annoying dream. The fact that she'd slept at all annoyed her, because it pointed to a physical weakness she detested. She'd slept for fourteen hours the night before. Surely that had been enough. And to dream of *Neil*?

She'd been right in her early assessment of him; he was as troubled as she was. She found herself pondering the specifics of his problem, then pushed those ponderings from her mind. She had her own problems. She didn't need his.

What she needed, she decided, was a cup of coffee. After the breakfast fiasco, she hadn't had either the courage or the desire to tackle coffee grounds, baskets and filters. Now, though, the thought of drinking something hot and aromatic appealed to her.

Levering herself awkwardly to her feet, she went into the kitchen and shook the coffeepot. He'd said there was some left but that it was thick. She didn't like thick coffee. Still, it was a shame to throw it out.

Determinedly she lit the gas and set the coffee on to heat.

Meanwhile, Neil was in the den, staring out the window at the rain, trying to understand himself. Deirdre Joyce—the young man who'd answered at Thomas's house had supplied her last name—was a thorn in his side. He wanted to be alone, yet she was here. It was midafternoon. He still hadn't spoken with Thomas, which meant that Deirdre was going to be around for another night at least.

What annoyed him most were the fleeting images that played tauntingly in the corners of his mind. A smooth, lithe back...a slim waist...the suggestion of a curve at the hip...a fresh, sweet scent...hair the color of wheat, not mousy brown as he'd originally thought, but thick, shining wheat. Her face, too, haunted him. She had the prettiest light-brown eyes, a small, almost delicate nose, lips that held promise when she smiled.

Of course, she rarely smiled. She had problems. And the fact of the matter was that he really did want to be alone. So why was he thinking of her in a way that would suggest that he found her attractive?

From the door came the clearing of a throat. "Uh, excuse me?"

He turned his head. Damn, but the mint-green of her warm-up suit was cheerful. Of course, she still looked lumpy as hell. "Yes?"

"I heated up the last of the coffee, but it really is too strong for me. I thought you might like it." Securing her right crutch with the muscles of her upper arm, she held out the cup.

Neil grew instantly wary. It was the first attempt she'd made at being friendly. Coming after nonstop termagancy, there had to be a reason. She had to want something. "Why?" he asked bluntly.

"Why what?"

"Why did you heat it up?"

She frowned. "I told you. I thought you might like it."

"You haven't been terribly concerned with my likes before."

"And I'm not now," she replied defensively. "It just seemed a shame to throw it out."

"Ah. You're making a fresh pot, so you heated the dregs for me."

"I don't believe you," she breathed. She hadn't expected such instant enmity, and coming in the face of her attempted pleasantness, it set her off. "You would have had me drink the dregs, but suddenly they're not good enough for you?"

"I didn't say they weren't good enough." His voice was smooth, with an undercurrent of steel. "I reheat coffee all the time because it saves time, and yes, it is a shame to throw it out. What I'm wondering is why the gesture of goodwill from you. You must have something up your sleeve."

"Boy," she remarked with a wry twist of her lips, "have *you* been burned."

His eyes darkened. "And just what do you mean by that?"

"For a man to be as suspicious of a woman, he'd have to have been used by one, and used badly."

Neil thought about that for a minute. Funny, it had never occurred to him before, but he had been used. Nancy had been crafty—subtle enough so the fact had registered only subliminally in his brain—but crafty nonetheless. Only now did he realize that often she'd done small things for him when she'd wanted something for herself. It fit in with the nature of her love, yet he hadn't seen it then. Just as he hadn't seen the potential for treachery at Wittnauer-Douglass.

"My history is none of your damned business," he ground out angrily.

"Fine," she spat. "I just want you to know that it's taken a monumental effort on my part to get the dumb coffee in here without spilling it. And if you want to know the truth, my major motivation was to find out where you were so I'd know what room to avoid." She set the mug on a nearby bookshelf with a thud. "You can have this or not. I don't care." She turned to leave, but not fast enough to hide the hint of hurt in her expression.

"Wait."

She stopped, but didn't turn back. "What for?" she asked. "So you can hurl more insults at me?"

He moved from the window. "I didn't mean to do that. You're right. I've been burned. And it was unfair of me to take it out on you."

"Seems to me you've been taking an awful lot out on me."

"And vice versa," he said quietly, satisfied when she looked over her shoulder at him. "You have to admit that you haven't been the most congenial of housemates yourself."

"I've had . . . other things on my mind."

He took a leisurely step closer. "So have I. I've needed to let off steam. Yelling at you feels good. It may not be right, but it feels good."

"Tell me about it," she muttered rhetorically, but he took her at face value.

"It seems that my entire life has been ruled by reason and restraint. I've never spouted off quite this way about things that are really pretty petty."

She eyed him askance. "Like my using the master bedroom?"

"Now that's not petty. That's a practical issue."

"Then what about heat? The bedroom is freezing, while the rest of the house is toasty warm. You purposely kept the thermostat low in that room, didn't you?"

"I told you. I like a cool bedroom."

"Well, I like a warm one, and don't tell me to use one of the other bedrooms, because I won't. You'll be leaving—"

"You'll be leaving." His voice had risen to match the vehemence of hers, but it suddenly dropped again. "Only problem is that Thomas still isn't in, so it looks like it won't be today."

"He's avoiding us."

"That occurred to you, too, hmm?"

"Which means that we're stranded here." Glumly she looked around. "I mean, the house is wonderful. Look." She gestured toward one wall, then another. "Hundreds of books to choose from, a stereo, a VCR, a television—"

"The TV reception stinks. I tried it."

"No loss. I hate television."

"Like you hate movies?"

"I didn't say I hated movies, just that lately they've been awful. The same is true of television. If it isn't a corny sit-com, it's a blood-and-guts adventure show, or worse, a prime-time soap opera."

"Opinionated urchin, aren't you?"

Her eyes flashed and she gripped her crutches tighter. "Yes, I'm opinionated, and I'm in the mood to express every one of those opinions." Silently she dared him to stop her.

Neil had no intention of doing that. He was almost curious as to what she'd say next. Reaching for the mug she'd set down, he leaned against the bookshelf, close enough to catch the fresh scent that emanated from her. "Go on. I'm listening."

Deirdre, too, was aware of the closeness, aware of the breadth of his shoulders and the length of his legs, aware of the fact that he was more man than she'd been near for a very long time. Her cheeks began to feel warm, and there was a strange tickle in the pit of her stomach.

Confused, she glanced around, saw the long leather couch nearby, and inched back until she could sink into it. She raked her lip with her teeth, then looked up at him. "What was I saying?"

"You were giving me your opinion of the state of modern television."

"Oh." She took a breath and thought, finally saying, "I hate miniseries."

"Why?"

"They do awful things to the books they're adapted from."

"Not always."

"Often enough. And they're twice as long as they need to be. Take the opening part of each installment. They kill nearly fifteen minutes listing the cast, then reviewing what went before. I mean, the bulk of the viewers know what went before, and it's a waste of their time to rehash it. And as for the cast listings, the last thing those actors and actresses need is more adulation. Most of them are swellheaded as it is!" She was warming to the subject, enjoying her own perversity. "But the worst part of television has to be the news."

"I like the news," Neil protested.

"I do, too, when it is news, but when stations have two hours to fill each night, a good half of what they deliver simply isn't news. At least, not what I'd consider to be news. And as for the weather report, by the time they've finished with their elaborate electronic maps and radar screens, I've tuned out, so I miss the very forecast I wanted to hear."

"Maybe you ought to stick to newspapers."

"I usually do."

"What paper do you read?"

"The *Times*."

"New York?" He was wondering about her connection to Victoria. "Then you live there?"

"No. I live in Providence."

"Ah, Providence. Thriving little metropolis."

"What's wrong with Providence?"

"Nothing that a massive earthquake wouldn't fix." It was an exaggeration that gave him pleasure.

She stared hard at him. "You probably know nothing about Providence, much less Rhode Island, yet you'd stand there and condemn the entire area."

"Oh, I know something about Providence. I represented a client there two years ago, in the middle of summer, and the air conditioning in his office didn't work. Since it was a skyscraper, we couldn't even open a window, so we went to what was supposed to be the in restaurant. The service was lousy, the food worse, and to top it all off, some bastard sideswiped my car in the parking lot, so I ended up paying for that, too, and *then* my client waited a full six months before settling my bill."

Deirdre was curious. "What kind of client?"

"I'm a lawyer."

"A lawyer!" She pushed herself to the edge of the seat. "No wonder you're not averse to criminals on the lecture circuit. The proceeds could well be paying your fee!"

"I am not a criminal attorney," Neil stated. The crease between his brows grew pronounced. "I work with corporations."

"That's even worse! I hate corporations!"

"You hate most everything."

Deirdre's gaze remained locked with his for a moment. He seemed to be issuing a challenge, asking a question about her basic personality and daring her to tell the truth. "No," she said in a quieter tone. "I'm just airing certain pet peeves. I don't—I can't do it very often."

He, too, had quieted. "What do you do?"

"Hold it in."

"No. Work-wise. You do work, don't you? All modern women work."

Deirdre dipped one brow. "There's no need for sarcasm."

He made no apology. "You pride yourself on being a modern woman. So tell me. What do you do for a living?"

Slowly she gathered her crutches together. She couldn't tell him what she did; he'd have a field day with it. "That—" she rose "—is none of your business."

"Whoa. I told you what I do."

"And I told you where I live. So we're even." Leaning into the crutches, she headed for the door.

"But I want to know what kind of work you do."

"Tough."

"I'll bet you don't work," he taunted, staying close by her side. "I'll bet you're a very spoiled relative of one of Victoria's very well-to-do friends."

"Believe what you want."

"I'll bet you're here because you really wanted to be in Monte Carlo, but Daddy cut off your expense account. You're freeloading off Victoria for a while."

"Expense account?" She paused midway through the living room and gave a brittle laugh. "Do fathers actually put their twenty-nine-year-old daughters on expense accounts?"

Neil's jaw dropped. "Twenty-nine. You're pulling my leg."

"I wouldn't pull your leg if it were attached to Mel Gibson!" she vowed, and continued on into the kitchen.

"Twenty-nine? I would have given you twenty-three, maybe twenty-four. But twenty-nine?" He stroked the stubble on his face and spoke pensively. "Old enough to have been married at least once." He started after her. "Tell me you're running away from a husband who beats you. Did he cause the broken leg?"

"No."

"But there is a husband?"

She sent him an impatient look. "You obviously don't know Victoria very well. She'd never have thrown us together if one of us were already married."

He did know Victoria, and Deirdre was right. "Okay. Have you ever been married?"

"No."

"Are you living with someone?" When she sent him a second, even more impatient look, he defended himself. "It's possible. I wouldn't put it past Victoria to try to get you to forget him if he were a creep. . . . Okay,

okay. So you're not living with someone. You've just broken up with him, and you've come here to lick your wounds."

"Wrong again." Seth had left four months before, and there had been no wounds to lick. Propping her crutches in a corner, she hopped to the cupboard. She was determined to make herself a cup of coffee. "This is sounding like *Twenty Questions*, which reminds me of what I *really* hate, and it's game shows like the one Thomas was watching yesterday. I mean, I know why people watch them. They play along, getting a rush when they correctly guess an answer before the contestant does. But the contestants—jumping all over the place, clapping their hands with glee when they win, kissing an emcee they don't know from Adam . . ." She shook her head. "Sad. Very sad."

Neil was standing close, watching her spoon coffee into the basket. Her hands were slender, well formed, graceful. There was something about the way she tipped the spoon that was almost lyrical. His gaze crept up her arm, over one rather nondescript shoulder to a neck that was anything but nondescript. It, too, was graceful. Strange, he hadn't noticed before. . . .

Momentarily suspending her work, Deirdre stared at him. Her eyes were wider than normal; her pulse had quickened. It occurred to her that she'd never seen so many textures on a man—from the thick gloss of his hair and the smooth slope of his nose to the furrowing of his brow and the bristle of his beard. She almost wanted to touch him . . . almost wanted to touch . . .

She tightened her fingers around the spoon. "Neil?"

He met her gaze, vaguely startled.

"I need room. I'm, uh, I'm not used to having someone around at home."

His frown deepened. "Uh, sure." He took a step back. "I think I'll . . . go take a walk or something."

Deirdre waited until he'd left, then slowly set back to work. *Take a walk. In the rain?* She listened, but there was no sound of the door opening and closing. So he was walking around the house. As good an activity as any to do on such a dismal day. She wondered when the rain would end. The island would be beautiful in sunshine. She'd love to go outside, find a high rock to sit on, and relax.

Surprisingly, when she thought of it, she wasn't all that tense, at least not in the way she'd been when she'd left Providence. In spite of the hassles of getting here, even in spite of the rain, the change of scenery was good for her. Of course, nothing had changed; Providence would be there when she returned. Her mother would be there, as would Sandra and the uncles. They'd be on her back again, unless she thought of some way to get them off.

She hadn't thought that far yet.

Carefully taking the coffee and a single crutch, she made her way into the den. She could put some weight on the cast without discomfort, which was a reassuring discovery. Carrying things such as coffee became a lot easier. Of course, it was a slow trip, and that still annoyed her, but it was better than being stuck in bed.

Leisurely sipping the coffee, she sat back on the leather sofa. Her duffel bag held several books, yarn and knitting needles, plus her cassette player and numerous tapes. None of these diversions appealed to her at the moment. She felt in limbo, as though she wouldn't completely settle down until Neil left.

But would he leave? Realistically? No. Not willingly. Not unless Victoria specifically instructed him to. Which she wouldn't.

Victoria had been clever. She'd known she was dealing with two stubborn people. She'd also known that once on the island, Neil and Deirdre would be virtually marooned. Thomas Nye was their only link with the mainland, and Thomas, while alert to any legitimate physical emergency, appeared to be turning a deaf ear to their strictly emotional pleas.

It was Neil and Deirdre versus the bad guys. An interesting prospect.

On impulse, she set down her cup and limped from the den. The house was quiet. She wondered what Neil was doing and decided that it was in her own best interest to find out. He hadn't returned to the living room while she'd been in the den, and he wasn't in the kitchen.

He was in the bedroom. The master bedroom. Deirdre stopped on the threshold and studied him. He lay on his back on the bed, one knee bent. His arm was thrown over his eyes.

Grateful she hadn't yet been detected, she was about to leave, when the whisper of a sound reached her ears. It was a little louder than normal breathing, a little softer than snoring. Neil was very definitely asleep.

Unable to help herself, she moved quietly forward until she stood by his side of the bed. His chest rose and fell in slow rhythm; his lips were faintly parted. As she watched, his fingers twitched, then stilled, and correspondingly something tugged at her heart.

He was human. When they'd been in the heat of battle, she might have tried to deny that fact, but seeing him now, defenseless in sleep, it struck her deeply. He was tired, perhaps emotionally as well as physically.

She found herself once again wondering what awful things he'd left behind. He was a lawyer; it was a good profession. Had something gone wrong with his career? Or perhaps his troubles related to his having been burned by a woman. Maybe he was suffering the effects of a bad divorce, perhaps worrying about children the marriage may have produced.

She actually knew very little about him. They'd been thrown together the moment she'd arrived at Spruce Head, and he'd simply provided a convenient punching bag on which to vent her frustrations. When she was arguing with him, she wasn't thinking of her leg, or aerobics, or Joyce Enterprises. Perhaps there was merit to his presence, after all.

He really wasn't so bad; at times she almost liked him. Moreover, at times she was physically drawn to him. She'd never before had her breath taken away by a man's nearness, but it had happened several times with Neil. For someone who'd always been relatively in control of her emotions, the experience was frightening. It was also exciting in a way....

Not trusting that Neil wouldn't awaken and lash out at her for disturbing him, she silently left the room and returned to the den. Her gaze fell on the ship-to-shore radio. She approached it, eyed the speaker, scanned the instructions for its use, then turned her back on both and sank down to the sofa. Adjusting one of the woven pillows beneath her head, she yawned and closed her eyes.

It was a lazy day. The sound of the rain was hypnotic, lulling, inducing the sweetest of lethargies. She wondered at her fatigue and knew that it was due only in part to her physical debilitation. The tension she'd been under in Providence was also to blame.

She needed the rest, she told herself. It was good for her. Wasn't that what a remote island was for? Soon enough she'd feel stronger, and then she'd read, knit, listen to music, even exercise. Soon enough the sun would come out, and she'd be able to avail herself of the island's fresh air.

But for now, doing nothing suited her just fine.

She was sleeping soundly when, some time later, Neil came to an abrupt halt at the door to the den. He was feeling groggy, having awoken only moments before. He wasn't used to sleeping during the day. He wasn't used to doing nothing. Oh, he'd brought along some books, and there were tapes here and a vast collection of old movies to watch, but he wasn't up to any of that just yet. If the weather were nice, he could spend time outdoors, but it wasn't, so he slept, instead.

Rationally he'd known that it was going to take him several days to unwind and that he badly needed the relaxation. He'd known that solutions to his problems weren't going to suddenly hit him in the face the moment he reached the island. Nevertheless, the problems were never far from consciousness.

Ironically Deirdre was his greatest diversion.

Deirdre. Looking down at her, he sucked in his upper lip, then slowly released it. Twenty-nine years old. He thought back to when he was that age. Four years out of law school, he'd been paying his dues as an associate in a large Hartford law firm. The hours had been long, the work boring. Frustrated by the hierarchy that relegated him to doing busywork for the partners, he'd set out on his own the following year. Though the hours had been equally long, the work had been far more rewarding.

Now, ten years later, he was approaching forty, sadly disillusioned. He knew where he'd been, saw his mistakes with vivid clarity... but he couldn't picture the future.

If Deirdre was disillusioned about something at the age of twenty-nine, where would she be when she reached his age? What did she want from life? For that matter, what had she had?

Lying there on her side, with her hands tucked between her thighs and her cheek fallen against the pillow, she was the image of innocence. She was also strangely sexy-looking.

He wondered how that could be, when there was nothing alluring about her in the traditional sense. She wore no make-up. Her hair was long in front, short at the sides and back, unsophisticated as hell. Her warm-up suit was a far cry from the clinging things he'd seen women wearing at the racquet club. The bulky fabric was bunched up in front, camouflaging whatever she had by the way of breasts, and yet... and yet... the material rested on a nicely rounded bottom—he could see that now—and she looked warm and vaguely cuddly. He almost envied her hands.

With a quick headshake, he walked over to the ship-to-shore radio, picked up the speaker, shifted it in his hand, frowned, then set it back down. Ah, hell, he told himself, Thomas wouldn't be there; he was conspiring with Victoria. Short of a legitimate physical emergency, he wouldn't be back soon. And that being the case, it behooved Neil to find a way to coexist in relative peace with Deirdre.

But what fun would that be?

Deirdre was, for him, a kind of punching bag. He felt better when he argued with her. She provided an outlet and a diversion. Perhaps he should just keep swinging.

Smiling, he sauntered into the living room. His gaze fell on the fireplace; the ashes from last night's fire lay cold. Taking several large logs from the nearby basket, he set them atop kindling on the grate and stuck a match. Within minutes the kindling caught, then the logs. Only when the fire was crackling heatedly did he settle back in a chair to watch it.

Strange, he mused, but he'd never come to the wilderness to relax before. He'd been to the beach—southern Connecticut, Cape Cod, Nantucket—and to the snow-covered mountains of Vermount. He'd been to the Caribbean and to Europe. But he'd never been this isolated from the rest of the world. He'd never been in the only house on an island, dependent solely on himself to see to his needs.

Nancy would die here. She'd want the option of eating out or calling room service. She'd want there to be people to meet for drinks. She'd want laundry service.

And Deirdre? Broken leg and all, she'd come looking for solitude. Perhaps stupidly, with that leg, but she'd come. Was she indeed a spoiled brat who had run away from all that had gone wrong in her life? Or was she truly self-sufficient? It remained to be seen whether she could make a bed....

"Nice fire."

He looked up. Deirdre was leaning against the wall by the hall, looking warm and still sleepy and mellow. He felt a lightening inside, then scowled perversely. "Where's the other crutch?"

Her eyes grew clearer. "In the kitchen."

"What's it doing there?"

She tipped her chin higher. "Holding up the counter."

"It's supposed to be under your arm. You're the one who needs holding up."

"I've found I can do just fine with one."

"If you put too much strain on the leg," he argued, "you'll slow the healing process."

"You sound like an expert."

"I broke my own leg once."

"How?"

"Skiing."

She rolled her eyes. "I should have guessed. I'll bet you sat around the ski lodge with your leg on a pedestal—the wounded hero basking in homage."

"Not quite. But what I did is beside the point. What you're doing is nuts. The doctor didn't okay it, did he?"

"*She* told me to use common sense. And what's it to you, anyway? You're not my keeper."

"No, but it'll be my job to do something if you fall and crack the cast, or worse, break the other leg."

She smiled smugly. "If anything happens to me, your problems will be solved. You'll get through to Thomas, zip, zip, and he'll be out to fetch me before you can blink an eye."

Neil knew she was right. He also knew that she had momentarily one-upped him. That called for a change of tactics. He took a deep breath, sat back in his chair and propped his bare feet on the coffee table. "But I don't want him to come out and fetch you. I've decided to keep you."

Her smile faded. "You've what?"

"I've decided to keep you."

"Given the fact that you don't *have* me, that's quite a decision."

He waved a hand. "Don't argue semantics. You know what I mean."

She nodded slowly. "You've decided to let me stay."

"That's right."

"And if I decide I want to leave?"

"Thomas won't give us the time of day, so it's a moot point."

"Precisely, which means that you're full of hot air, Neil Hersey. You can't decide to keep me, any more than I can decide to keep you, or either of us can decide to leave. We're stuck here together, which means—" Her mind was working along pleasurable lines. The grin she sent him had a cunning edge. "That you're stuck with me, bad temper and all." The way she saw it, he'd given her license to fire at will, not to mention without guilt. Battling with him could prove to be a most satisfying pastime.

"I think I can handle it," he said smugly.

"Good." Limping directly between Neil and the fire, she took the chair opposite his. "So," she said, sitting back, "did you have a good sleep?"

"You spied on me?"

"No. I walked into my bedroom and there you were. Snoring."

He refused to let her get to him. "Is that why you took your nap in the den?"

"You spied on me."

"No. I walked in there intending to call Thomas. Then I decided not to bother. So I came in here and built a fire. It is nice, isn't it?"

"Not bad." She levered herself from the chair and hopped into the kitchen. A bowl of fresh fruit sat on the counter; she reached for an orange, then hopped back to her seat.

"You're a wonderful hopper," Neil said. "Is it your specialty?"

She ignored him. "What this fire needs is a little zip." Tearing off a large wad of orange peel, she tossed it into the flame.

"Don't do that! It'll mess up my fire!"

"It adds a special scent. Just wait." She threw in another piece.

Neil stared into the flames. "I hate the smell of oranges. It reminds me of the packages of fruit my grandparents used to send up from Florida every winter. There was so much of it that my mother worried about it spoiling, so we were all but force-fed the stuff for a week." His voice had gentled, and his lips curved at the reminiscence. "Every year I got hives from eating so many oranges."

She pried off a section and held it ready at her mouth. "You said 'we.' Do you have brothers and sisters?" The orange section disappeared.

"One of each."

"Older or younger?"

"Both older."

"Are you close?"

"Now? Pretty close." He shifted lower in his seat, so that his head rested against its back, and crossed his ankles. "We went our separate ways for a while. John is a teacher in Minneapolis, and Sara works for the government in Washington. They're both married and have kids, and all our lives seemed so hectic that we really didn't push reunions."

"What changed that?" Deirdre asked.

"My mother's death. Something about mortality hit us in the face—you know, life-is-so-short type of thing. That was almost seven years ago. We've been much closer since then."

"Is your father still living?"

"Yes. He's retired."

"Does he live near you?"

"He still lives in the house where we grew up in Westchester. We keep telling him to move because it's large and empty but for him most of the time. He won't sell." Neil was grinning. "He travels. So help me, nine months out of twelve he's galavanting off somewhere. But he says he needs the house. He needs to know it's there for him to come home to. Personally—" he lowered his voice "—I think he just doesn't want to displace the couple who live above the garage. They've been overseeing the grounds for nearly twenty years. They oversee *him* when he's around, and he loves it."

Absently Deirdre pressed another piece of fruit into her mouth. She chewed it, all the while looking at Neil. It was obvious that he felt affection for his family. "That's a lovely story. Your father sounds like a nice man."

"He is."

She took a sudden breath. "So how did he get a son like you? By the way, aren't your feet freezing? I haven't seen you with socks on since we got here, but it's cold."

He wiggled his toes. "I'm warm-blooded."

"You're foolhardy. You'll get splinters."

"Are you kidding? The floor's been sanded and waxed. Only the walls have splinters, and, thank you, I don't walk on walls." He swung his legs down and stood. "So you'll have to find something else to pick on me for."

"I will," she promised. "I will." She watched him escape into the kitchen. "What are you doing?"

"Contemplating dinner."

"We haven't had lunch!"

"Breakfast was lunch." He flipped on a light in the darkening room. "Now it's dinnertime."

She glanced at her watch. It was well after six o'clock. She supposed she was hungry, though the thought of preparing another meal was enough to mute whatever hunger pangs she felt. So she remained where she was, looking at the fire, telling herself that she'd see to her own needs when Neil was done. She didn't want an audience for her clumsiness. Besides, between her hopping and Neil's size, they'd never be able to work in the kitchen at the same time.

She listened to the sounds of his preparations, wondering how he'd come to be so handy. Various possible explanations passed through her mind, but in the end the question remained. Then she heard the sizzle of meat and began to smell tantalizing aromas, and her admiration turned to annoyance. Why *was* he so good in the kitchen? Why wasn't he as clumsy as she? The men she'd known would have been hollering for something long before now—help in finding the butter or sharpening a knife or preparing vegetables for cooking. Why didn't he need her for something?

Pushing herself from the chair, she limped peevishly to the kitchen. What she saw stopped her cold on the threshold. Neil had set two places at the table and was in the process of lowering one brimming plate to each spot.

He looked up. "I was just about to call you." Her expression of shock was ample reward for his efforts, though his motives went deeper. If he helped Deirdre with things he knew she found difficult, he wouldn't feel so badly when he picked on her. Good deeds for not-so-good ones; it seemed a fair exchange. Not to mention the fact that keeping her off balance seemed of prime importance. "Steak, steamed broccoli, dinner rolls." He beamed at the plates. "Not bad, if I do say so myself."

"Not bad," she echoed distractedly. "You'd make someone a wonderful wife."

He ignored the barb and held out her chair. "Ms Joyce?"

At a loss for anything better to do, particularly when her mouth was watering, she came forward and let him seat her. She stared at the attractive plate for a minute, then looked up as he poured two glasses of wine. "Why?" she asked bluntly.

"Why wine? It's here for us to drink, and I thought it'd be a nice touch.

"Why me? I didn't ask you to make my dinner."

"Are you refusing it?"

She glanced longingly at her plate. Hospital food was nearly inedible; it had been days since she'd confronted anything tempting. "No. I'm hungry."

"So I figured."

"But you must have something up your sleeve."

He sat at his place, nonchalantly shook out his napkin and spread it on his lap. "Maybe I'm thinking of Victoria's kitchen. You broke a glass this morning. Another few, and we'll run low."

"It's not the glass, and you know it. What is it, Neil? I don't like it when you're nice."

He arched a brow as he cut into his steak. "Prefer the rough stuff, do you? A little pushing and shoving turns you on?" He put a piece of steak into his mouth, chewed it and closed his eyes. "Mmmm. Perfect." His eyes flew open in mock innocence. "I hope you like it rare."

"I like it medium."

"Then you can eat the edges and leave the middle." He gestured with his fork. "Go ahead. Eat. On second thought—" he set down the fork and reached for his wine "—a toast." When Deirdre continued to stare at him, he dipped his head, coaxing. "Come on. Raise your glass."

Slowly, warily, she lifted it.

He grinned. "To us." The clink of his glass against hers rang through the room.

5

TO US. Deirdre thought about that through the evening as she sat pensively before the fire. She thought about it that night when she lay in bed, trying her best to ignore the presence of a large male body little more than an arm's length away. She thought about it when she awoke in the morning. By that time she was annoyed.

Victoria had fixed them up. Deirdre had always resented fix-ups, had always fervently avoided them. She'd never been so hard up for a man that she'd risk taking pot luck, and she wasn't now. Who was Neil Hersey, anyway? She asked herself that for the umpteenth time. After spending thirty-six hours with the man, she still didn't know. She did know that she'd been aware of him in some form or another for the majority of those thirty-six hours, and that her body was distinctly tense from that awareness.

She turned her head to study him. Sleeping, he was sprawled on his back with his head facing her. His hair was mussed; his beard sported an additional day's growth. Sooty eyelashes fanned above his cheekbones. Dark swirls of hair blanketed his chest to the point where the quilt took over.

One arm was entirely free of the covers. Her gaze traced its length, from a tightly muscled shoulder, over a leanly corded swell to his elbow, down a forearm that was spattered with hair, to a well-formed and thoroughly masculine hand. As though touched by that hand, she felt a quiver shoot through her.

Wrenching her head to the other side, she took a shallow breath, pushed herself up and dropped her legs over the side of the bed. For a minute she simply sat there with her head bowed, begrudging the fact that she found Neil attractive. She wanted to hate the sight of him after what he'd done to her dreams of solitude. But the sight of him turned her on.

She didn't want to be turned on.

Slowly she began to roll her head in a half circle, concentrating on relaxing the taut muscles of her neck. She extended the exercise to her shoulders, alternately rolling one, then the other. Clasping her hands at the back of her head, she stretched her torso, first to the left, then to the right. The music played in her mind, and she let herself move to its sound, only then realizing what she'd missed during the past week, finding true relaxation in imagining herself back at the health club, leading a class.

"What in the hell are you doing?" came a hoarse growl from behind her.

Startled from her reverie, she whirled around, then caught herself and tempered the movement. "Exercising."

"Is that necessary?"

"Yes. My body is tense."

"So is mine, and what you're doing isn't helping it." He'd awoken with the first of her exercises and watched her twist and stretch, watched the gentle shift in her absurdly large pajamas. And he'd begun to imagine things, which had quickly affected his own body. In other circumstances he'd have stormed from bed right then. As things stood—literally—he didn't have the guts.

"Then don't look," she said, turning her back on him and resuming her exercises. It was spite that drove her on, but all petty thoughts vanished when a strong arm seized her waist and whipped her back on the bed. Before she knew what had happened, Neil had her pinned and was looming over her.

"I think we'd better get something straight," he warned in a throaty voice. "I'm a man, and I'm human. If you want to tempt me beyond my limits, you'd better be prepared to take the consequences."

Deirdre's trouble with breathing had nothing to do with exercising. Neil's lunge had dislodged the quilt, leaving his entire upper body bare. The warmth of his chest reached out to her, sending rivulets of heat through her body, while the intensity of his gaze seared her further.

"I didn't know you were tempted," she said in a small voice. "I'm a bundle of lumps to you. That's all." She'd been a bundle of lumps to most men, lumps that were conditioned by steady exercise, lumps that were anything but feminine. She'd always known she couldn't compete with the buxom beauties of the world, and she fully assumed Neil was used to buxom beauties. The way he'd looked at her that first day had left no doubt as to his opinion of her body. Then again, there had been other times when he'd looked at her . . .

"You are a bundle of lumps," he agreed, dropping his gaze to her pajama front. "That's what's so maddening. I keep wondering what's beneath all this cover." His eyes made a thorough survey of the fabric—she felt every touch point—before lazily meeting hers. "Maybe if I see, I won't be tempted. Maybe what we need here is full disclosure."

Deirdre made a reflexive attempt at drawing in her arms to cover herself, but he had them anchored beneath his and gave no quarter.

"Maybe," he went on, his voice a velvety rasp, "what I ought to do is to unbutton this thing and take a good look at all you're hiding."

"There's not much," she said quickly. Her eyes were round in a pleading that she miraculously managed to keep from her voice. "You'd be disappointed."

"But at least then I wouldn't have to wonder anymore, would I?"

Her heart was hammering, almost visibly so. She was frightened. Strangely and suddenly frightened. "Please. Don't."

"Don't wonder? Or don't look?"

"Either."

"But I can't help the first."

"It's not worth it. Take my word for it. I'm an athletic person. Not at all feminine."

Neil was staring at her in growing puzzlement. He heard the way her breath was coming in short bursts, saw the way her eyes held something akin to fear. He felt the urgency in his body recede, and slowly, gently he released her. Instantly, she turned away from him and sat up.

"I'd never force you," he murmured to her rigid back.

"I didn't say you would."

"You were talking, rationalizing as though you thought I would. I scared you."

She said nothing to that. How could she explain what she didn't understand herself: that her fear had been he'd find fault with her body? She didn't know why it should matter what he thought of her body. . . .

"You didn't scare me."

"You're lying."

"Then that's another fault to add to the list." She fumbled for her crutches and managed to get herself to her feet. "I'm hungry," she grumbled, and started for the door.

"So am I," was his taunting retort.

"Tough!"

DEIRDRE MADE her own breakfast, grateful to find such easy fixings as yogurt and cottage cheese in the refrigerator. She waited in the den until she heard Neil in the kitchen, then retreated to the other end of the house for a bath.

At length she emerged, wearing the same bulky green top she'd worn during the drive up. This time she had gray sweatpants on, and though the outfit didn't clash, it was less shapely than yesterday's warm-up suit had been.

Reluctant to face Neil, she busied herself cleaning up the bedroom. Making a king-size bed by hobbling from one side to the other and back took time, but for once she welcomed the handicap. She went on to unpack her duffel bag. It wasn't that she hadn't planned on staying, simply that she hadn't had the strength to settle in until now. Yes, she did feel stronger, she realized, and found some satisfaction in that. She also found satisfaction in placing her books, cassette player and tapes atop the dresser. Neil had put his things on the other dresser; she was staking her own claim now.

Under the guise of housekeeping, she crossed to that other dresser and cursorily neatened Neil's things. He'd brought several books, a mix of fiction and nonfiction, all tied in some fashion to history. A glass case lay nearby, with the corner of a pair of horn-rimmed spectacles protruding. Horn-rimmed spectacles. She grinned.

Completing the gathering on the dresser was a scattered assembly of small change, a worn leather wallet and a key ring that held numerous keys in addition to those to his car. She wondered what the others unlocked, wondered where his office was and what it was like, wondered where he lived.

Moving quickly into the bathroom, she wiped down the sink and shower, then the mirror above the sink. She'd put her own few things in one side of the medicine chest. Curious, she slid open the other side. Its top shelf held a number of supplies she assumed were Victoria's. Far below, after several empty shelves, were more personal items—a comb, a brush, a tube of toothpaste and a toothbrush.

Neil's things. He traveled light. There was no sign of a razor. He'd very obviously planned to be alone.

Strangely, she felt better. Knowing that Neil was as unprepared for the presence of a woman as she was for the presence of a man was reassuring. On the other hand, what would she have brought if she'd known she'd have company? Makeup? Aside from mascara, blusher and lip gloss, she rarely used it. A blow dryer? She rarely used one. Cologne? Hah!

And what would Neil have brought? She wondered.

Sliding the chest shut with a thud, she returned to the bedroom, where a sweeping glance told her there was little else to clean. She could always stretch out on the bed and read, or sit in the chaise by the window and knit. But that would be tantamount to hiding, and she refused to hide.

Discouraged, she looked toward the window. It was still raining. Gray, gloomy and forbidding. If things were different, she wouldn't have been stopped by the rain; she'd have bundled up and taken a walk. All too clearly, though, she recalled how treacherous it was maneuvering with crutches across the mud and rocks. She wasn't game to try it again soon.

Selecting a book from those she'd brought, she tucked it under her arm alongside the crutch, took a deep breath and headed for the living room. Neil was there, slouched on the sofa, lost in thought. He didn't look up until she'd settled herself in the chair, and then he sent her only the briefest of glances.

Determinedly she ignored him. She opened the book, a piece of contemporary women's fiction and began to read, patiently rereading the first page three times before she felt justified in moving on to the second. She was finally beginning to get involved in the story, when Neil materialized at her shoulder.

Setting the book down, she turned her head, not far enough to see him, just enough to let him know he had her attention. "Something wrong?" she asked in an even tone.

"Just wondering what you were reading," he said just as evenly.

Leaving a finger to mark her place, she closed the cover so he could see it.

"Any good?" he asked.

"I can't tell yet. I've just started."

"If it doesn't grab you within the first few pages, it won't."

"That's not necessarily true," she argued. "Some books take longer to get into."

He grunted and moved off. She heard a clatter, then another grunt, louder this time, and, following it, a curse that brought her head around fast. "Goddamn it. Can't you keep your crutches out of the way?" He had one hand on the corner of her chair, the other wrapped around his big toe.

"If you were wearing shoes, that wouldn't have happened!"

"I shouldn't have to wear shoes in my own home."

"This isn't your own home."

"Home away from home, then."

"Oh, please, Neil, what exactly would you have me do? Leave the crutches in the other room? You were the one who was after me to use them."

He didn't bother to answer. Setting his foot on the floor, he gingerly tested it. Then he straightened and limped across the room to stand at the window. He tucked his hands in the back pockets of his jeans, displacing the long jersey that would have otherwise covered his buttocks. The jersey itself was black and slim cut, fairly broadcasting the strength and breadth of his shoulders, the leanness of his hips. She wondered if he'd chosen to wear it on purpose.

Returning her eyes to her book, she read another two pages before being interrupted again.

"Crummy day" was the information relayed to her from the window.

She set the book down. "I know."

"That's two in a row."

"Three."

"Two full days that we've been here."

She conceded the point. "Fine. Two in a row." She picked up the book again. Several pages later, she raised her head to find Neil staring at her. "Is something wrong?"

"No."

"You look bored."

"I'm not used to inactivity."

"Don't you have anything to do?"

With a shrug he turned back to the window.

"What would you do at home on a rainy day?" she asked.

"Work."

"Even on a weekend?"

"Especially on a weekend. That's when I catch up on everything I've been too busy to do during the week." At least, it had been that way for years, he mused. Of course, when one was losing clients right and left, there was a definite slackening.

"You must have a successful practice," she remarked, then was taken aback when he sent her a glower. "I meant that as a compliment."

He bowed his head and rubbed the back of his neck. "I know. I'm sorry."

Deirdre glanced at her book, and realized she wasn't going to get much reading done with Neil standing there that way. She was grateful he hadn't made reference to what had happened earlier, and wondered if he was sorry for that, too. If so, she reflected, he might be in a conciliatory mood. It was as good a time as any to strike up a conversation.

"How do you know Victoria?" she asked in as casual a tone as she could muster.

"A mutual friend introduced us several years ago."

"Are you from the city?"

"Depends what city you mean."

For the sake of civility, she stifled her impatience. "New York."

"No." He was facing the window again, and for a minute she thought she'd have to prod, when he volunteered the information she'd been seeking. "Hartford."

A corner of her mouth curved up. She couldn't resist. "Ah, Hartford. Thriving little metropolis. I went to a concert there last year with friends. The seats were awful, the lead singer had a cold and I got a flat tire driving home."

Slowly Neil turned. "Okay. I deserved that."

"Yes, you did. Be grateful I didn't condemn the entire city."

He wasn't sure he'd have minded if she had. At the moment he felt the whole of Hartford was against him. "My allegiance to the city isn't blind. I can see her faults."

"Such as . . . ?"

"Parochialism. Provinciality."

"Hartford?"

"Yes, Hartford. Certain circles are pretty closed."

"Isn't that true of any city?"

"I suppose." Casually he left the window and returned to the sofa. Deirdre took it as a sign of his willingness to talk.

"Have you lived there long?"

"Since I began practicing."

"You mentioned going to school in Boston. Was that law school, or undergraduate?"

"Both."

"So you went from Westchester to Boston to Hartford?"

He had taken on an expression of amused indulgence. "I did a stint in San Diego between Boston and Hartford. In the Navy. JAG division."

"Ah. Then you missed Vietnam."

"Right." He had one brow arched, as though waiting for her to criticize the fact that he hadn't seen combat.

"I think that's fine," she said easily. "You did something, which is more than a lot of men did."

"My motive wasn't all that pure. I would have been drafted if I hadn't signed up."

"You could have run to Canada."

"No."

The finality with which he said it spoke volumes. He felt he'd had a responsibility to his country. Deirdre respected that.

"How did you break your leg?" he asked suddenly.

The look on her face turned sour. "Don't ask."

"I am."

She met his gaze and debated silently for a minute. He'd opened up. Perhaps she should, too. Somehow it seemed childish to continue the evasion. She gave him a challenging stare. "I fell down a flight of stairs."

He held up a hand, warding off both her stare and its unspoken challenge. "That's okay. I'm not laughing."

Averting her gaze, she scowled at the floor. "You would if you knew the whole story."

"Try me. What happened?"

She'd set herself up for it, but strangely she wasn't sorry. It occurred to her that she wanted to tell the story. If he laughed, she'd have reason to yell at him. In some ways, arguing with him was safer than...than what had happened earlier.

Taking a breath, she faced him again. "I slipped on a magazine, caught my foot in the banister and broke my leg in three places."

He waited expectantly. "And...? There has to be a punch line. I'm not laughing yet."

"You asked what I did for a living." She took a breath. "I teach aerobic dance."

His eyes widened fractionally. "Ah. And now you can't work."

"That's the least of it! I've always been into exercise of one sort or another. I'm supposed to be ultracoordinated. Do you have any idea how humiliating it is to have done this slipping on a magazine?"

"Was the magazine worth it?" he asked, deadpan.

"That's not the point! The point is that I'm not supposed to fall down the stairs! And if I do, I'm supposed to do it gracefully, with only a black-and-blue mark or two to show for it." She glared at her leg. "Not a grotesque cast!"

"How does the leg feel, by the way?"

"Okay."

"The dampness doesn't bother it?"

"My thigh is more sore from lugging the cast around, and my armpits hurt from the crutches."

"That'll get better with time. How long will the cast be on?"

"Another five weeks."

"And after that you'll be good as new?"

Her anger was replaced by discouragement. "I wish I knew. The doctor made no promises. Oh, I'll be able to walk. But teach?" Her shrug was as eloquent as the worry in her eyes.

Neil surprised himself by feeling her pain. Wasn't it somewhat akin to his own? After all, his own future was in limbo, too.

Leaning forward, he propped his elbows on his thighs. "You'll be able to teach, Deirdre. One way or another you will, if you want to badly enough."

"I do! I have to work. I mean, it's not a question of money. It's a question of emotional survival!"

That, too, he understood. "Your work means that much to you."

It was a statement, not a question, and Deirdre chose to let it rest. She wasn't ready to go into the issue of Joyce Enterprises, which was so much more complex and personal. Besides, Neil was a corporate attorney. He'd probably take *their* side.

"Well," she said at last, "I guess there's nothing I can do but wait."

"What will you do in the meantime?"

"Stay here for as long as I can."

"There's nothing else to keep you busy in Providence while your leg mends?"

"Nothing I care to do."

Neil wondered at her mutinous tone, but didn't comment. "What had you planned to do here? Besides read."

Still scowling, she shrugged. "Relax. Knit. Listen to music. Work up some routines. It may be a waste of time if it turns out I can't teach, but I suppose I have to hope."

"You could have done all that in Providence. I'd have thought that with a broken leg and all, you'd be more comfortable there. The drive up couldn't have been easy, and if Thomas had dumped you on that dock alone, you'd have had a hell of a time getting everything to the house."

Her scowl deepened. "Thomas knew what he was doing. *You* were here. Otherwise he'd probably have helped me himself."

"Still, to rush up here the day you left the hospital . . . What was the rush?"

"The telephone! My family! It was bad enough when I was in the hospital. I had to get away!"

"All that, just because you were embarrassed?"

Deirdre knew that she'd be spilling the entire story in another minute. Who in the devil was Neil Hersey that he should be prying? She hadn't asked *him* why he'd been in such a foul mood from day one. "Let's just say that I have a difficult family," she concluded, and closed her mouth tightly. Between that and the look she gave him, there was no doubt that she was done talking.

Neil took the hint. Oh, he was still curious, but there was time. Time for . . . lots of things.

She opened her book again and picked up where she'd left off, but if her concentration had been tentative before, it was nonexistent now. She was thinking of that difficult family, wondering what was going to change during the time she was in Maine that would make things any better when she returned.

From the corner of her eye she saw Neil get up, walk aimlessly around the room, then sit down. When a minute later he bobbed up again, she sighed.

"Decide what you want to do, please. I can't read with an active yo-yo in the room."

He said nothing, but took off for the bedroom. Moments later he returned, threw himself full length on the sofa and opened a book of his own. He read the first page, turned noisily to the last, then began to flip through those in between.

"Are you going to read or look at the pictures?" Deirdre snapped.

His face was the picture of innocence when he looked up. "I'm trying to decide if it's worth reading."

She was trying to decide if he was purposely distracting her. "You brought it along, didn't you?"

"I was in a rush. I took whatever books I had around the house and threw them in the bag."

"Then you must have decided it was worth reading when you bought it. What's it about?" She wondered which he'd chosen.

"World War I. History fascinates me."

"I know."

His eyes narrowed. "How would you know?"

"Because I saw the books lying on your dresser, and every one of them dealt with history in some form. You know, you really should wear your glasses when you read. Otherwise you'll get eye strain."

"I only wear them when I *have* eye strain, and since I haven't had much to look at for the past two days, my eyes are fine." He turned his head on the sofa arm to study her more fully. "You're pretty nosy. Did you look through my wallet, too?"

"Of course not! I was cleaning, not snooping. I've never liked living in a pigpen."

"Could've fooled me, what with the way you've been dropping clothes around."

"That was only the first night, and I was exhausted." She noticed a strange light in his eyes and suspected he was enjoying the sparring. It occurred to her that she was, too. "What's in your wallet, anyway? Something dark and sinister? Something I shouldn't see?"

He shrugged. "Nothing extraordinary."

"Wads of money?"

"Not quite."

"A membership card to a slinky men's club?"

"Not quite."

"A picture of your sweetheart?"

"Not . . . quite."

"Who is she, anyway—the one who burned you?"

The day before he wouldn't have wanted to talk about Nancy. Now, suddenly, it seemed less threatening. "She's someone I was seeing, whom I'm not seeing now."

"Obviously," Deirdre drawled. "What happened?"

Neil pursed his lips and thought of the best way to answer. He finally settled on the most general explanation. "She decided I didn't have enough potential."

"What was she looking for? An empire builder?"

"Probably."

"You don't sound terribly upset that she's gone."

"I'm getting over it," he said easily.

"Couldn't have been all that strong a relationship, then."

"It wasn't."

Deirdre settled her book against her stomach and tipped her head to the side. "Have you ever been married?"

"Where did that come from?"

"I'm curious. You asked me. Now I'm asking you."

"No. I've never been married."

"Why not?"

He arched a brow. "I never asked you that. It's impolite."

"It's impolite to ask a woman that, because traditionally she's the one who has to wait for the proposal. A man can do the proposing. Why haven't you?"

It occurred to Neil that there was something endearing about the way Deirdre's mind worked. It was quick, unpretentious, oddly refreshing. He smiled. "Would you believe me if I said I've been too busy?"

"No."

"It is true, in a way. I've spent the past fifteen years devoted to my career. She's a very demanding mistress."

"Then she's never had the right competition, which means that the old cliché is more the case. You haven't met the right woman yet."

He didn't need to ponder that to agree. "I have very special needs," he said, grinning. "Only a very special woman can satisfy them."

Deirdre could have sworn she saw mischief in his grin. She tried her best to sound scornful. "That I can believe. Any woman who'd put up with a face full of whiskers has to be special. Do you have any idea how . . . how grungy that looks?"

The insult fell flat. To her dismay, he simply grinned more broadly as he stroked his jaw. "It does look kinda grungy. Nice, huh?"

"Nice?"

"Yeah. I've never grown a beard in my life. From the time I was fifteen I shaved every blessed morning. And why? So I'd look clean. And neat. And acceptable. Well, hell, it's nice to look grungy for a change, and as for acceptability—" He searched for the words he wanted, finally thrust out his chin in defiance. "Screw it!"

Deirdre considered what he'd said. He didn't look unclean, or unneat, or unacceptable, but rather . . . dashing. Particularly with that look of triumph on his face. Helpless against it, she smiled. "That felt good, didn't it?"

"Sure did."

"You're much more controlled when you work."

"Always. There's a certain, uh, decorum demanded when you're dealing with corporate clients."

"Tell me about it," she drawled, bending her right leg up and hugging it to her chest.

Once before, he'd taken her up on the offer. This time he let it ride, because he didn't really want to talk about corporate clients. He wanted to talk about Deirdre Joyce.

"What about you, Deirdre? Why have you never married?"

"I've never been asked."

He laughed. "I should have expected you'd answer that way. But it's a cop-out, you know," he chided, then frowned and tucked in his chin. "Why are you looking at me that way?"

"Do you know that that's the first time I've heard you laugh, I mean, laugh, as in relaxed and content?"

His smile mellowed into something very gentle, and his eyes bound hers with sudden warmth. "Do you know that's the first time I've heard such a soft tone from you. Soft tone, as in amiable." As in womanly, he might have added, but he didn't. He'd let down enough defenses for one day.

For a minute Deirdre couldn't speak. Her total awareness centered on Neil and the way he was looking at her. He made her feel feminine in a way she'd never felt before.

Awkward, she dropped her gaze to her lap. "You're trying to butter me up, being nice and all. I think you're looking for someone to do the laundry."

Laundry was the last thing on his mind. "I don't think I've ever seen you blush before."

The blush deepened. She didn't look up. She didn't trust the little tricks her hormones were playing on her. She felt she was being toasted from the inside out. It was a new and unsettling sensation. Why *Neil*?

Lips turning down in a pout, she glared at him.

"Aw, come on," he teased. "I liked you the other way."

"Well, I didn't." It smacked of vulnerability, and Deirdre didn't like to think of herself as vulnerable. "I'm not the submissive type."

His laugh was gruffer this time. "I never thought you were. In fact, submissive is the last word I'd use to describe you. You prickle at the slightest thing. I'd almost think that *you*'d been burned."

The directness of her gaze held warning. "I have. I was used once, and I didn't like the feeling."

"No one does," he said softly. "What happened?"

She debated cutting off the discussion, but sensed he'd only raise it another time. So she crossed her right leg over her cast and slid lower in the chair in a pose meant to be nonchalant. "I let myself be a doormat for a fellow who had nothing better to do with his life at the time. The minute he sensed a demand on my part, he was gone."

"You demanded marriage?"

"Oh, no. It was nothing like that. Though I suppose he imagined that coming. My family would like to see me married. They don't think much of my...life-style."

"You're a swinger?"

She slanted him a disparaging glance. "Just the opposite. I avoid parties. I can't stand phony relationships. I hate pretense of any kind."

"What does pretense have to do with marriage?"

"If it's marriage for the sake of marriage alone, pretense is a given."

Neil couldn't argue with that. "Do you want to have children?"

"Someday. How about you?"

"Someday."

They looked at each other for a minute longer, then simultaneously returned to their books. Deirdre, for one, was surprised that she was talking about these things with Neil. She asked herself what it was about him that inspired her to speak, and finally concluded that it was the situation, more than the man, that had brought her out. Hadn't she come here to soul-search, to ponder the direction her life was taking?

Neil was brooding about his own life, his own direction, and for the first time that brooding was on a personal bent. Yes, he'd like to be married, but only to the right person. He was as averse to pretense as Deirdre was. Nancy—for that matter, most of the women he'd dated over the years—had epitomized pretense. One part of him very much wanted to put his law practice in its proper perspective, to focus, instead, on a relationship with a woman, a relationship that was intimate, emotionally as well as physically, and rewarding. And yes, he'd like to have children.

Absently he turned a page, then turned it back when he realized he hadn't read a word. He darted a glance at Deirdre and found her curled in the chair, engrossed in her book. She was honest; he admired her for that. She didn't have any more answers than he did, but at least she was honest.

Settling more comfortably on the sofa, Neil refocused on his book and disciplined himself to read. It came easier as the morning passed. The rain beat a steady accompaniment to the quiet activity, and he had to admit that it was almost peaceful.

Setting the book down at last, he stood. "I'm making sandwiches. Want one?"

Deirdre looked up. "What kind?"

His mouth turned down at the corner. "That's gratitude for you, when someone is offering to make you lunch."

"I can make my own," she pointed out, needing to remind him—and herself—that she wasn't helpless.

"Is that what you'd rather?"

"It depends on what kind of sandwiches you know how to make."

"I know how to make most anything. The question is what have we got to work with?" He crossed into the kitchen, opened the refrigerator and rummaged through the supplies. Straightening, he called over his shoulder, "You can have ham and cheese, bologna and cheese, grilled cheese, grilled cheese and tomato, grilled cheese and tuna, a BLT, egg salad, peanut butter and jelly, cream cheese and jelly—" he sucked in a badly needed breath "—or any of the above taken separately."

Any of the above sounded fine to Deirdre, who'd never been a picky eater. She tried not to grin. "That's quite a list. Could you run through it one more time?"

The refrigerator door swung shut and Neil entered her line of vision. His hands were hooked low on his hips and his stance was one of self-assurance. "You heard it the first time, Deirdre."

"But there are so many things to choose from . . . and it's a big decision." She pressed her lips together, feigning concentration. "A big decision . . ."

"Deirdre . . ."

"I'll have turkey with mustard."

"Turkey wasn't on the list."

"No? I thought for sure it was."

"We don't have any turkey."

"Why not? Thomas should have known to pick some up. Turkey's far better for you than ham or cheese or peanut butter."

Hands falling to his sides, Neil drew himself up, shoulders back. He spoke slowly and clearly. "Do you, or do you not, want a sandwich?"

"I do."

"What kind?"

"Grilled cheese and tuna."

He sighed. "Thank you." He'd no sooner returned to the refrigerator, when he heard her call.

"Can I have it on rye?"

"No, you cannot have it on rye," he called back through gritted teeth.

"How about a roll?"

"If a hamburg roll will do."

"It won't."

"Then it's white bread or nothing. Take it or leave it."

"I'll take it."

He waited a minute longer to see if she had anything else to add. When she remained silent, he tugged open the refrigerator and removed everything he'd need. He'd barely closed the door again, when Deirdre entered the kitchen.

"If you've changed your mind," he warned, "that's tough. Your order's already gone to the cook. It's too late to change."

She was settling herself on the counter stool. "Grilled cheese and tuna's fine." Folding her hands in her lap, she watched him set to work.

He opened a can of tuna, dumped its contents into a bowl and shot her a glance as he reached for the mayonnaise. A glob of the creamy white stuff went the way of the tuna. He was in the process of mixing it all together with a fork, when he darted her another glance. "Anything wrong?"

"No, no. Just watching. You don't mind, do you? I'm fascinated. You're very domestic for a man."

"Men have to eat."

"They usually take every shortcut in the book, but grilled cheese and tuna . . . I'm impressed."

"It's not terribly difficult," he scoffed.

"But it takes more time than peanut butter and jelly."

"Tastes better, too."

"I *love* peanut butter and jelly."

"Then why'd you ask for grilled cheese and tuna?"

She arched a brow, goading him on. "Maybe I wanted to see what you could do."

Neil, who'd been slathering tuna on slices of bread, stopped midstroke, put down the knife and slowly turned. "You mean you purposely picked what you thought was the hardest thing on the menu?"

Deirdre knew when to back off. "I was only teasing. I really do feel like having grilled cheese and tuna."

With deliberate steps, he closed the small distance between them. "I don't believe you. I think you did it on purpose, just like you asked for turkey when you knew damn well we didn't have it."

She would have backed up if there'd been anywhere to go, but the counter was already digging into her ribs. "Really, Neil." She held up a hand. "There's no need to get upset. Unless you're having ego problems with my being in the kitchen this way—"

The last word barely made it from her mouth, when Neil scooped her up from the stool, cast and all, and into his arms.

"What are you doing?" she cried.

He was striding through the living room. "Removing you from my presence. You wanted to get my goat. Well, you got it. Picking the most complicated sandwich. *Ego* problems." They were in the hall and moving steadily. "If you want to talk, you can do it to your heart's content in here." He entered the bedroom and went straight to the bed, his intent abundantly clear to

Deirdre, who was clutching the crew neckline of his jersey.

"Don't drop me! My cast!"

Neil held her suspended for a minute, enjoying the fact of his advantage over her. Then, in a single heartbeat, his awareness changed. No longer was he thinking that she'd goaded him once too often. Rather, he was suddenly aware that her thigh was slender and strong beneath one of his hands, and that the fingertips of the other were pressed into an unexpectedly feminine breast. He was thinking that her eyes were luminous, her lips moist, her cheeks a newly acquired pale pink.

Deirdre, too, had caught her breath. She was looking up at Neil, realizing that his eyes, like her hair, weren't black at all, but a shade of charcoal brown, and that his mouth was strong, well formed and very male. She was realizing that he held her with ease, and that he smelled clean, and that the backs of her fingers were touching the hot, hair-shaded surface of his chest and he felt good.

Slowly he lowered her to the bed, but didn't retreat. Instead he planted his hands on either side of her. "I don't know what in the hell is going on here," he breathed thickly. "It must be cabin fever." His gaze fell from her eyes to her lips, declaring his intent even before he lowered his head.

6

HIS MOUTH TOUCHED hers lightly at first, brushing her lips, sampling their shape and texture. Then he intensified the kiss, deepening it by bold degrees until it had become something positively breathtaking.

Deirdre could barely think, much less respond. She'd known Neil was going to kiss her, but she'd never expected such force in the simple communion of mouths. He drank from her like a man who was dying of thirst, stumbling unexpectedly upon an oasis in the desert. From time to time his lips gentled to a whisper, touching hers almost timidly in reassurance that what he'd found wasn't a mirage.

His hands framed her face, moving her inches away when his mouth would have resisted even that much. "Kiss me, Deirdre," he breathed, studying her through lambent eyes.

His hoarse command was enough to free her from the spell she'd been under. When he brought her mouth back to his, her lips were parted, curious, eager, and she returned his kiss with growing fervor. She discovered the firmness of his lips, the evenness of his teeth, the texture of his tongue. She tasted his taste and breathed his breath, and every cell in her that was woman came alive.

"Deirdre," he whispered, once again inching her face from his. He pressed his warm forehead to hers and worked at catching his breath. "Why did you *do* that?"

Deirdre, who was having breathing difficulties of her own, struggled to understand. "What?"

"Why did you do that?"

"Do what?"

"Kiss me!"

The haze in her head began to clear, and she drew farther away. "You told me to kiss you."

His brows were drawn together, his features taut. "Not like that. I expected just a little kiss. Not . . . not that!"

He was angry. She couldn't believe it. "And who was kissing whom first like that?"

His breath came roughly, nostrils flaring. "You didn't have to do it back!" Shoving his large frame from the bed, he stormed from the room, leaving Deirdre unsure and bewildered and, very quickly, angry.

She sat up to glare in the direction he'd gone, then closed her eyes and tried to understand his reaction. Though she'd never, never kissed or been kissed that way, she wasn't so inexperienced that she couldn't see when a man was aroused. Neil Hersey had been aroused, and he'd resented it.

Which meant he didn't want involvement any more than she did.

Which meant they had a problem.

She'd enjoyed his kiss. More than that. It had taken her places she'd never been before. Kissing Neil had been like sampling a rich chocolate with a brandy center, sweet and dissolving—yet potent. He went straight to her head.

She touched her swollen lips, then her tingling chin. Even his beard had excited her, its roughness a contrast to the smoothness of his mouth. Yes, he was smooth. Smooth and virile and stimulating, damn him!

Dropping her chin to her chest, she took several long, steadying breaths. With the fresh intake of oxygen came the strength she needed. Yes, they were stuck under the same roof. They were even stuck, thanks to a matching stubbornness, in the same bed. She was simply going to have to remember that she had problems enough of her own, that *he* had problems enough of his own. And that he could be a very disagreeable man.

Unfortunately Neil chose that moment to return to the bedroom. He carried her crutches and wore an expression of uncertainty. After a moment's hesitation on the threshold, he started slowly toward the bed.

"Here," he said, quietly offering the crutches. "The sandwiches are under the broiler. They'll be ready in a minute."

Deirdre met his gaze, then averted her own, looking to the crutches. She reached for them, wrapped her hands around the rubber handles and studied them for a minute before raising her eyes again.

The corners of his mouth curved into the briefest, most tentative of smiles before he turned and left the room.

Leaning forward, Deirdre rested her head against the crutches. Oh, yes, Neil was a very disagreeable man. He also had his moments of sweetness and understanding, which, ironically, was going to make living with him that much more of a trial.

She sighed. It had to be done. Unless she was prepared to capitulate and leave the island by choice. Which she wasn't.

Struggling to her feet, she secured the crutches under her arms and, resigned, headed for the kitchen.

Lunch was a quiet, somewhat awkward affair. Neil avoided looking at Deirdre, which she had no way of knowing, since she avoided looking at him. She complimented him on the sandwiches. He thanked her. When they were done, he made a fresh pot of coffee—medium thick—and carried a cup to the living room for her. She thanked him. And all the while she was thinking of that kiss, as he was. All the while she was wondering where it might have led, as he was. All the while she was asking herself why, as was he.

Knowing she'd never be able to concentrate on her book, she brought her knitting bag from the bedroom, opened the instruction booklet and forced her attention to the directions.

Neil, who was in a chair drinking his second cup of coffee, was as averse to reading as she was, but could think of nothing else he wanted to do. "What are you making?" he asked in a bored tone.

She didn't look up. "A sweater."

"For you?"

"Hopefully." She reached for a neatly wound skein of yarn, freed its end and pulled out a considerable length. Casting on—that sounded simple enough.

Neil noted the thick lavender strand. "Nice color."

"Thank you." With the book open on her lap, she took one of the needles and lay the strand against it.

"That's a big needle."

She sighed. Concentration was difficult, knowing he was watching. "Big needle for a big sweater."

"For you?"

Her eyes met his. "It's going to be a bulky sweater."

"Ah. As in ski sweater?"

She pressed her lips together in angry restraint. "As in warm sweater, since it looks like I won't be skiing in the near future."

"Do you ski?"

"Yes."

"Are you good?"

She dropped the needle to her lap and stared at him. "I told you I was athletic. I exercise, play tennis, swim, ski . . . At least, I used to do all of those things. Neil, I can't concentrate if you keep talking."

"I thought knitting was an automatic thing."

"Not when you're learning how."

One side of his mouth twitched. "You haven't done it before?"

"No, I haven't."

"Was it the broken leg that inspired you?"

"I bought the yarn several months ago. This is the first chance I've had to work with it."

He nodded. She lifted the needle again, studied the book again, brought the yarn up and wound it properly for the first stitch. It took several attempts before she'd made the second, but once she'd caught on, she moved right ahead. Before long she had enough stitches cast on to experiment with the actual knitting.

When Neil finished his coffee, he returned the cup to the kitchen and started wandering around the house. At last, all else having failed to divert him, he picked up his book again.

By this time Deirdre was painstakingly working one knit stitch after another. The needles were awkward in her hands, and she continually dropped the yarn that was supposed to be wrapped around her forefinger. Periodically she glanced up to make sure Neil wasn't witnessing her clumsiness, and each time she was frowning when she returned to her work. Simply looking at him turned her inside out.

He was stretched full length on the couch...so long...so lean. The sleeves of his jersey were pushed back to reveal forearms matted with the same dark hair she'd felt on his chest. *Felt.* Soft, but strong and crinkly. The texture was permanently etched in her memory.

From his position on the sofa, Neil was also suffering distractions. His curiosity as to what Deirdre hid beneath her bulky sweatshirt had never been greater. He'd felt the edge of her breast. *Felt.* Strong and pert, but yielding beneath his fingertips. He'd carried her; she was light as thistledown and every bit as warm. He'd tasted her. That was his worst mistake, because there'd been a honeyed sweetness to her that he never would have imagined. Did the rest of his imaginings pale by comparison to the real thing?

From beneath half-lidded eyes he slanted her a look. Her hands gripped the needles, the forefinger of each extended. She was struggling, he saw, but even then the sweep of her fingers was graceful. Athletic? Perhaps. But if so, in a most healthy, most fitting, most feminine way.

Slapping the book shut, he sat bolt upright. Deirdre's questioning eyes shot to him.

"I can't read with that clicking," he grumbled. "Can't you be any quieter?"

"I'm having trouble as it is. Do you want miracles?"

"Not miracles. Just peace and quiet." Dropping the book on the sofa, he began to prowl the room.

"Book didn't grab you?"

"No." He ran a hand through his hair. "How about playing a game? Victoria has a bunch of them in the other room."

The knitting fell to Deirdre's lap. She wasn't sure she was up to playing games with Neil. "What did you have in mind?" she asked warily.

"I don't know. Maybe Monopoly?"

"I hate Monopoly. There's no skill involved."

"What about Trivial Pursuit?"

"I'm no good at history and geography. They make me lose."

"You make you lose," he argued. "The game doesn't do it."

"Whatever. The result's the same."

"Okay. Forget Trivial Pursuit. How about chess?"

"I don't know how."

"Checkers."

She scrunched up her nose in rejection.

"Forget a game," he mumbled.

"How about a movie?" she asked. It was a rainy day; the idea held merit. Her fingers were cramped, anyway.

"Okay."

"What do we have to choose from?"

In answer he started off toward the den. Deirdre levered herself up and followed, finding him bent over a low shelf in contemplation of the video tapes. She came closer, trying not to notice how snugly his jeans molded his buttocks, how they were slightly faded at the spot where he sat.

"*Magnum Force?*" he suggested.

"Too violent."

"*North by Northwest?*"

"Too intense." Leaning over beside him, she studied the lineup. "How about *Against All Odds?*"

"That's a romance."

"So?"

"Forget it."

"Then *The Sting*. Unromantic, but amusing."

"And boring. The best part's the music."

Her gaze moved across the cassettes, eyes suddenly widening. "*Body Heat*. That's a super movie. William Hurt, Kathleen Turner, intrigue and—"

"—Sex." Neil's head was turned, eyes boring into her. "I don't think we need that."

He was right, of course. She couldn't believe she'd been so impulsive as to suggest that particular movie.

"Ah." He drew one box out. "Here we go. *The Eye of the Needle*. Now that was a good flick."

It had action, intrigue, and yes, a bit of sex, but Deirdre felt she could take it. "Okay. Put it on." She set her crutches against the wall and hopped to the leather couch.

Removing the cassette from its box, Neil inserted it in the VCR, pressed several buttons, then took the remote control and sank onto the couch an arm's length from Deirdre. The first of the credits had begun to roll, when he snapped it off and jumped up.

"What's wrong?" she asked.

"We need popcorn. I saw some in the kitchen cabinet."

"But it takes time to make popcorn, and we're all set to watch."

"We've got time. Besides, it doesn't take more than a couple of minutes in the microwave." He rubbed his hands together. "With lots of nice melted butter poured on top—"

"Not butter! It's greasy, and awful for you."

"What's popcorn without butter?" he protested.

"Healthier."

"Then I'll put butter on mine. You can have yours without."

"Fine." She crossed her arms over her chest and sat back while he went to make the popcorn. Gradually her frown softened. It was rather nice being waited on, and Neil wasn't complaining. She supposed that if she'd had to be marooned with a man, she could have done worse. She *knew* she could have done worse. She could have been stuck with a real egomaniac. True, Neil had his moments. It occurred to her that while she'd given him a clue as to what caused her own mood swings, as yet she had no clue to his motivation. She'd have to work on that, she decided, merely for the sake of satisfying her curiosity. Nothing else.

Neil entered the room carrying popcorn still in its cooking bag. He resumed his seat, turned the movie back on and positioned the bag at a spot midway between them.

"Did you add butter?" she asked cautiously.

"No. You're right. I don't need it."

"Ah. Common sense prevails."

"Shh. I want to watch the movie."

She glanced at the screen. "I'm only disturbing the credits."

"You're disturbing me. Now keep still."

Deirdre kept still. She reached for a handful of popcorn and put one piece, then another in her mouth. The movie progressed. She tried to get into it but failed.

"It's not the same watching movies at home," she remarked. "A theater's dark. It's easier to forget your surroundings and become part of the story."

"Shh." Neil was having trouble of his own concentrating. It wasn't the movie, although as he'd seen it before, it held no mystery. What distracted him was Deirdre sitting so close. Only popcorn separated them. Once, when he reached into the bag, his hand met hers. They both retreated. And waited.

"You go first," he said.

She kept her eyes on the small screen. "No. That's okay. I'll wait."

"I've already had more. Go ahead."

"I don't need it. I'll get fat."

"You won't get fat." From what he'd seen, she wasn't a big eater; as for getting fat, from what he'd felt she was slender enough. Still, he couldn't resist a gibe. "On second thought, maybe you're right. You will get fat. You're smaller than I am, and I'm the one who's getting all the exercise around here. I'll wear it off easier."

He reached for the popcorn, but Deirdre already had her hand in the bag. She withdrew a full fist, sent him a smug grin and with deliberate nonchalance popped several pieces into her mouth.

Neil, who'd almost expected she'd do just that, wasn't sure whether to laugh or scream. Deirdre was impetuous in a way that was adorable, and adorable in a way that was bad for his heart. She had only to look at him with those luminous brown eyes and his pulse raced. He never should have kissed her. Damn it, he never should have kissed her!

But he had, and that fact didn't ease his watching of the rest of the movie. He was constantly aware of her—aware when she shifted on the couch, aware when she dropped her head back and watched the screen through half-closed eyes, aware when she began to massage her thigh absently.

"Leg hurt?" he asked.

She looked sharply his way, then shrugged and looked back at the screen.

"Want some aspirin?"

"No."

"Some Ben-Gay?"

"There is no Ben-Gay."

His lips twitched. "I'd run to the island drugstore for some if you'd let me rub it on."

She glared at the movie, but carried on the farce. "The island drugstore's out. I checked."

"Oh. Too bad."

Deirdre clamped her lips tightly, silently cursing Neil for his suggestion. *Let me rub it on.* Her insides tingled with a heat that, unfortunately, didn't do a whit to help her thigh.

Neil, too, cursed the suggestion, because his imagination had picked up from there, and he'd begun to think of rubbing far more than her thigh. He wondered whether her breasts would fit his hand, whether the skin of her belly would be soft....

He shifted away from her on the couch, and made no further comments, suggestive or otherwise. The movie was ruined for him. He was too distracted to follow the dialogue; the intrigue left him cold; the sex left him hot. The only thing that brought him any relief from the build-up of need in his body was the thought of Hartford, of work, of Wittnauer-Douglass. And because that upset him all the more, he was truly between a rock and a very hard place, where he remained throughout the evening.

He and Deirdre ate dinner together. They sat together before the fire. They pretended to read, but from the way Deirdre's eyes were more often on the flames than her book, he suspected that she was accomplishing as little as he was. He also suspected that her thoughts were running along similar lines, if the occasional nervous glances she cast him were any indication.

There was an element of fear in her. He'd seen it before; he could see it now. And it disturbed him. Was she afraid of sex? Was she afraid of feeling feminine and heated and out of control?

Even as he asked himself those questions, his body tightened. What in the hell was *he* afraid of? Certainly not sex. But there was something holding him back, even when every nerve in his body was driving him on.

He sat up by the fire long after Deirdre had taken refuge in bed. When at last he joined her, he was tired enough to fall asleep quickly. By the time the new day dawned, though, he was wondering whether he should relent and sleep in another room. Twice during the night he'd awoken to find their bodies touching—his outstretched arm draped over hers, the sole of her foot nestled against his calf.

What *was* it that made them gravitate toward each other? Each had come to Maine in search of solitude, so he'd have thought they'd have chosen to pass the time in opposite corners of the house. That hadn't been the case. Spitting and arguing—be it in the bedroom, the kitchen, the living room or den—they'd been together. And now ... still ... the bed.

He saw Deirdre look over her shoulder at him, then curl up more tightly on her side. Rolling to his back, he stared up at the ceiling, but the image there was of a disorderly mop of wheat-colored hair, soft brown eyes still misty with sleep, soft cheeks bearing a bed-warmed flush and lips that were slightly parted, unsure, questioning.

He had to get out. Though there was still the intermittent patter of rain and the air beyond the window was thick with mist, he had to get out. Without another glance at Deirdre, he flew from the bed, pulled on the dirty clothes he'd been planning to wash that day, laced on the sneakers that still bore a crust of mud from the day of his arrival on the island, threw his Windbreaker over his shoulders and fled the room, then the house.

Surrounded by the silence left in his wake, Deirdre slowly sat up. Being closed in had finally gotten to him, she mused. It had gotten to her, too. Or was it Neil who'd gotten to her? She'd never spent as uncomfortable an evening or night as those immediately past, her senses sharpened, sensitized, focused in on every nuance of Neil's physical presence. He breathed; she heard it. He turned; she felt it. Once, when she'd awoken in the middle of the night to find her hand tucked under his arm, she'd nearly jumped out of her skin, and not from fear of the dark.

Her body was a coiled spring, taut with frustration. She wanted to run six miles, but couldn't run at all. She wanted to swim seventy-two laps, but couldn't set foot in a pool, much less the ocean. She wanted to exercise until she was hot and tired and dripping with sweat, but ... but ... Damn it, yes, she could!

Shoving back the covers, she grabbed her crutches, took a tank top and exercise shorts from the dresser drawer and quickly pulled them on. She sat on the bed to put on her one sock and sneaker and both leg warmers, then pushed herself back up, tucked her cassette player and several tapes under one arm and her crutch under the other, and hobbled into one of the spare bedrooms. Within minutes the sounds of Barry Manilow filled the house.

Deirdre took a deep breath and smiled, then closed her eyes and began her familiar flexibility exercises. Her crutches lay on the spare bed; she discovered she could stand perfectly well without them. And the fact that various parts of the routine had to be altered in deference to her leg didn't bother her. She was moving.

In time with the music, she did body twists and side bends. She stretched the calf and ankle muscles of her right leg, and the inner thigh muscles of both legs. It felt good, so good to be feeling her body again. She took her time, relaxed, let the music take her where it would.

After several minutes, she moved into a warm-up, improvising as she went to accommodate her limited mobility. The music changed; the beat picked up, and she ventured into an actual dance routine. Though she couldn't dance in the true sense of the word, her movements were fluid and involved her entire upper torso as well as her good leg. By the time she'd slowed to do a cool-down routine, she'd broken into a healthy sweat and felt better than she had in days.

So immersed was she in the exercise that she didn't hear the open and closing of the front door. Neil, though, heard her music the minute he stepped into the house. He was incensed; it was loud and far heavier than the music he preferred. Without bothering to remove his wet jacket, he strode directly toward the sound, intent on informing Deirdre that as long as they were sharing the house, she had no right to be so thoughtless.

He came to an abrupt halt on the threshold of the spare bedroom, immobilized by the sight that met him. Eyes closed, seeming almost in a trance, Deirdre was moving in time to the music with a grace that was remarkable given her one casted leg. But it wasn't the movement that lodged his breath in his throat. It was her. Her body.

If he'd wondered what she'd been hiding beneath her oversized clothes, he didn't have to wonder any longer. She wore a skimpy tank top that revealed slender arms and well-toned shoulders. Her breasts pushed pertly at the thin fabric, their soft side swells clearly visible when she moved her arms. Her waist was small, snugly molded by the elasticized band of her shorts, and the shorts themselves were brief, offering an exaggerated view of silken thighs.

He gave a convulsive swallow when she bent over, his eyes glued to crescents of pale flesh. Then she straightened and stretched, arms high over her head, dipping low and slow from one side to the other. He swallowed again, transfixed by the firmness of her breasts, which rose with the movement.

Neil realized then that Deirdre's shapelessness had belonged solely to her bulky sweat clothes. Deirdre Joyce was shapely and lithe. With her hair damp around her face, her skin gleaming under a sheen of perspiration, with her arms flexing lyrically, her breasts bobbing, her hips rocking, she looked sultry, sexy and feminine.

He was in agony. His own body was taut, and his breath came raggedly. Turning, he all but ran down the hall, through the master bedroom, directly into the bathroom. He was tugging at his clothes, fumbling in his haste, knowing only that if he didn't hit a cold shower soon he'd explode.

His clothing littered the floor, but he was oblivious to the mess. Stepping into the shower, he turned on the cold tap full force, put his head directly beneath the spray, propped his fists against the tile wall and stood there, trembling, until the chill of the water had taken the edge of fever from his body. He thought of Hartford, of Wittnauer-Douglass, of his uncle who'd died the year before, of basketball—anything to get his mind off Deirdre. Only when he felt he'd gained a modicum of control did he adjust the water temperature to a more comfortable level for bathing.

Deirdre, who was totally unaware of the trial Neil had been through, finished her cool-down exercises and did several final stretches before allowing herself to relax in a nearby chair. Feeling tired but exhilarated, she left the music on; it was familiar, comfortable and reassuring.

At length she sat forward and reached for her crutches, knowing that if she didn't dry off and change clothes, her perspiration-dampened body would soon be chilled.

She turned off the music and listened. The house was still silent, which meant, she reasoned, that Neil was still outside, which meant, she reasoned further, that she could have the bathroom to herself without fear of intrusion. A warm bath sounded very, very appealing.

The smile she wore as she swung her way down the hall was self-congratulatory. She was proud of herself. She'd exercised, and in so doing had not only proved that she could do it, but had worked off the awful tension she'd awoken with that morning. So much for Neil Hersey and his virility, she mused. She could handle it.

Intending to fill the tub while she undressed, she passed straight through the master bedroom to the bathroom. The door was closed. Without a thought, she shouldered it open and let the rhythm of her limp carry her several feet into the room. There she came to a jarring halt.

Neil stood at the sink. His head was bowed and he was bent slightly at the waist, his large hands curving around the edges of the porcelain fixture. He was stark naked.

The breath had left her lungs the instant she'd seen him, and Deirdre could do no more than stare, even when he slowly raised his head and looked at her. He had a more beautifully male body than she'd ever have dreamed. His back was broad and smooth, his flanks lean, his buttocks tight. Seen in profile, his abdomen was flat, his pelvic bones just visible beneath a casement of flesh, his sex heavy and distinct.

"Deirdre?" His voice was husky. Her eyes flew to his when, without apparent modesty, he straightened and turned to face her. Two slow steps brought him close enough to touch. He repeated her name, this time in a whisper.

She was rooted to the spot, barely able to breathe, much less speak. Her eyes were wide and riveted to his.

He brought up a hand to brush the dots of moisture from her nose, then let his thumb trail down her cheek, over her jaw to her neck and on to the quivering flesh that bordered the thin upper hem of her tank top. Her breath was suddenly coming in tiny spurts that grew even tinier when he slipped his hand beneath her shoulder strap and brushed the backs of his fingers lower, then lower. She bit her lip to stifle a cry when he touched the upper swell of her breast, and though she kept her eyes on his, she was aware of the gradual change in his lower body.

"I didn't know you looked like this," he said hoarsely. "You've kept it all hidden."

Deirdre didn't know what to say. She couldn't quite believe he was complimenting her, not when he was so superbly formed himself. Surely the other women who'd seen him this way had been far more desirable than she. And though she knew he was aroused, her insecurities crowded in on her.

The backs of his fingers were gently rubbing her, dipping ever deeper into her bra. "Take off your clothes," he urged in a rough murmur, eyes flaming with restrained heat. "Let me see you."

She shook her head.

"Why not?"

She swallowed hard and managed a shaky whisper. "I'm sweaty."

"Take a shower with me." His baby finger had reached the sensitive skin just above her nipple, coaxing.

Pressing her lips together to hold in a moan, she shook her head again. "I can't take a shower." Her voice was small, pleading.

"Then a bath. Let me bathe you."

She wasn't sure if it was the sensuality of his words, or the fact that his finger had just grazed the hard nub of her nipple, but her good knee buckled, and she would have fallen had not her crutches been under her arms. His finger moved again, then again, sending live currents through her body. This time she couldn't contain the soft moan that slipped from her throat.

"Feel good?" he whispered against her temple, his own breath coming quicker.

"I don't want it to," she cried.

"Neither do I, but it does, doesn't it?"

It felt heavenly—his touching her, his being so near, so naked. She wanted to be naked beside him, too, but she was frightened. He'd be disappointed. She was sure of it. She was an athlete, "boyish" by her family's definition, and that description had haunted her doggedly over the years. She wasn't soft and fragile and willowy.

And even if Neil wasn't disappointed looking at her, he'd be let down by what would come after that. She felt the ache, the emptiness crying out inside of her, and knew she'd want to make love. And then he'd be disappointed, and the illusion would be broken.

She hobbled back a step, dislodging his hand. "I have to go. I have to go, Neil." Without waiting for his reply, she turned and fled from the bathroom, taking refuge in the bedroom where she'd exercised, collapsing in the chair and cursing her failings. *So much for handling Neil's virility.* Hah!

She didn't know how long she sat there, but the sweat had long since dried from her skin and she was feeling chilled when Neil appeared at the door. He wore a fresh pair of jeans and a sweater, and was barefoot, as usual. She wished she could believe that things were back to normal between them, but she knew better.

Neil felt neither anger nor frustration as he looked at her, but rather a tenderness that stunned him. Padding slowly into the room, he took an afghan from the end of the bed, gently draped it over her shoulders, then came down on his haunches beside her chair. "What frightens you, Deirdre?" he asked in a tone that would have melted her if the sight of him hadn't already done so.

It was a minute before she could speak, and then only brokenly. "You. Me. I don't know."

"I'd never hurt you."

"I know."

"Then what is it? You respond to me. I can feel it in your body. Your breath catches, and you begin to tremble. Is that fear, too?"

"Not all of it."

"You do want me."

"Yes."

"Why don't you give in and let go? It'd be good between us."

She looked down at her hands, which were tightly entwined in her lap. "Maybe for me, but I'm not sure for you."

"Why don't you let me be the judge of that?"

"I'm an athlete, not soft and cuddly like some women."

"Just because you're athletic doesn't mean you're not soft and cuddly. Besides, if it was a cushiony round ball I wanted, I'd go to bed with a teddy bear."

As he'd intended, his comment brought a smile to her face. But it was a tentative smile, a nervous one. "Somehow I can't picture that."

"Neither can I, but, then, I can't picture myself being disappointed if you let me hold you...touch you...make love to you."

His words sent a ripple of excitement through her, and there was clear longing in her gaze as she surveyed his face. "I'm scared" was all she could manage to say.

Neil studied her a minute longer, then leaned forward and kissed her lightly. "I'd never hurt you. Just remember that." Standing, he left the room.

His words were in Deirdre's mind constantly as the day progressed. She believed that he'd meant what he'd said, but she knew that there were different kinds of hurt. Physical hurt was out of the question; Neil was far too gentle for that. But emotional hurt was something else. If their relationship should take the quantum leap that lovemaking would entail...and he should be let down...she'd be hurt. How it had happened, she didn't know, particularly since they'd spent most of their time together fighting, but Neil had come to mean something to her. She wasn't up to analyzing the exact nature of that something; all she knew was that she was terrified of endangering it.

If he'd thought long and hard, Neil couldn't have come up with a better way to goad Deirdre that day than by being kind, soft-spoken and agreeable. Without a word he prepared their meals. Without a word he did the laundry. He was indulgent when she tackled her knitting again, abiding the noise without complaint. He was perfectly amenable to watching her choice of movie on the VCR. He didn't start a single argument, but, then, neither did she. It was the quietest day they'd spent on the island.

Deirdre was as aware as he of that fact. She was also aware that, by denying her any cause to bicker, Neil was allowing her time to think about what he'd said and what she was going to do about it. If the issue had been entirely cerebral, she might have had a chance to resist him. But her senses refused to be reasoned with and were constantly attuned to his presence. That side of her she'd never paid much heed to was suddenly clamoring for attention. Though all was peaceful on the outside, inside she was a mass of cells crying for release from a tension that radiated through her body in ever-undulating waves.

By the time they'd finished dinner and had spent a quiet hour before the fire, she had her answer. Yes, she was frightened and very, very nervous, but she'd decided that if Neil approached her again, she wouldn't refuse him. The sensual side of her nature wouldn't allow her to deny herself.

Head bowed, she quietly got to her feet, secured her crutches under her arms and left the living room. Once in the bedroom, she slowly changed into her pajamas, then sat on the side of the bed and reviewed her decision. She was taking a chance, she knew. A big one. If things didn't go well, the atmosphere in the house would be worse than ever. Then again, maybe not. They might be able to settle into a platonic relationship for the rest of their time here. Then again, Neil might not even come to her....

Even as she pondered that possibility, she sensed his presence in the room. Her head swiveled toward the door, eyes following his silent approach. Every one of her insecurities found expression in her face. Her back was straight. Her hands clutched the rounded edge of the bed.

More than anything at that moment, Neil wanted to alleviate her fear. It tore at him, because he knew he was its cause, just as he knew that her fear was unfounded. If she worried that she wouldn't please him, she worried needlessly. Deirdre turned him on as no other woman had, turned him on physically and in a myriad of other ways he'd only begun to identify.

Hunkering down, he raised his eyes to hers. He wanted to ask, but couldn't find the words. One part of him was frightened, too—frightened of being turned down when the one thing he wanted, the one thing he needed just then, was to be accepted, to be welcomed. So his question was a wordless one, gently and soulfully phrased.

Deirdre's insides were trembling, but she wasn't so wrapped up in apprehension that she didn't hear his silent request. It was a plea that held its share of unsureness, and that fact, more than anything, gave her the courage she needed.

Of its own accord, her hand came up, touching his cheek, inching back until her fingers wove gently into his hair. Tentatively, nervously, she let her lips soften into the beginnings of a smile.

Neil had never seen anything as sweet. He felt relief, and a kind of victory. But more, a well of affection rose inside, spreading warmth through him. Whatever Deirdre's fears were, she was willing to trust him. That knowledge pleased him every bit as much as the prospect of what was to come.

Holding her gaze, he brought his hands up to frame her face. His thumbs stroked her lips for a minute before he came forward and replaced them with his mouth. His kiss was sure and strong, the sealing of a pact, but it was every bit as gentle in promise, and Deirdre was lost in it. It was almost a shock when he set her back and she remembered that there was more to lovemaking than kisses alone. Her expression reflected her qualms, and Neil was quick to reassure her.

"Don't be frightened," he whispered. "We'll take it slow." Sitting back on his haunches, he slid his hands to her neck, then lower to the first button of her pajamas, which he released. He moved on to the second button, working in such a way that some part of his hand constantly touched her flesh. For him, the touch point reflected sheer greed; for Deirdre it was a sensually electric connection that served as a counterpoint to her apprehension.

Only when the last of the buttons was released did Neil lower his gaze. With hands that trembled slightly, he drew back the voluminous pajama fabric, rolling it outward until her breasts were fully exposed. The sight of them, small and high, but well rounded, shook him deeply. He'd been right; imagination did pale against reality. Or maybe it was that he hadn't dared dream....

The cool air of the bedroom hit Deirdre simultaneously with trepidation, but when her arms would have moved inward, he gently held them still.

"You're beautiful, Deirdre," he breathed. "What could ever have made you think that you wouldn't be right for me?"

She didn't answer, because the light in his eyes was so special, so precious, that she was afraid of distracting him lest his fascination fade. So she watched, mesmerized, as he brought both hands to her breasts. Long fingers circled them, tracing only their contours before growing bolder. A soft sigh slipped through her lips when he began to knead her fullness, and the feeling was so right and so good that she momentarily forgot her fears.

When the pads of his fingers brushed her nipples, she stiffened her back, but it was a movement in response to the surge of heat, not a protest. She had to clutch his shoulders then, because he had leaned forward and opened his mouth over one tight nub, and the sensation was jolting her to her core.

His tongue dabbed the pebbled tip. His teeth toyed with it. And all the while his hand occupied her other breast, caressing it with such finesse that she bit her lip to keep from crying out.

At last, when she simply couldn't help herself, she began to whimper. "Neil . . . I don't think I can stand this. . . ."

"If I can, you can," he rasped against her skin.

"I feel like I'm on fire. . . ."

"You are."

"I can't sit still. . . ."

"Sure you can. Let it build."

"It's been building for three days!"

"But it has to be slow, has to be right."

He drew back only long enough to whip the sweater over his head. Then he came up to sit beside her and take her in his arms. That first touch, flesh to flesh, was cataclysmic. Deirdre's entire body shook when her breasts made contact with his chest. Her arms went around him, holding him tightly, as though otherwise she'd simply shatter.

Neil's grip on her was no less definitive. His large body shuddered at the feel of her softness pressing into it. His breath came raggedly by her ear, while his hands hungrily charted every inch of her bare back, from her shoulders, over her ribs, to the dimpled hollows below her waist. Her pajama bottoms hung around her hips; he took advantage of their looseness to explore the creamy smoothness of her belly, the flare of her hips, the conditioned firmness of her bottom.

Deirdre, whose body all but hummed its pleasure, was finding a second heaven touching Neil. She loved the broad sweep of his back, the textured hollows of his collarbone, the sinewed swells of his chest. Slipping her hands between their bodies, she savored his front as she'd done his back. It was hairier, enticingly so, and his nipples were every bit as taut, if smaller, than hers were.

"What you do to me, Deirdre," he murmured dazedly, recapturing her face with his hands and taking her lips in a fevered kiss. "I think I agree with you. I'm not sure how much more I can stand, either."

She'd been right, he realized. Though they hadn't known it at the time, they'd endured three days of foreplay. From the very first there'd been curiosity. And it had grown more intense, despite every argument they'd had, despite every scathing comment they'd exchanged. Later he would wonder how much of the fighting had been caused by that basic attraction between them, but for now all he could think about was that their mutual desire was on the verge of culmination.

Coming up on one knee, he grasped her under the arms and raised her gently to the pillow. He eased the quilt from under her until she was lying on the bare sheet, then, unsnapping her pajama bottoms, he worked them down her legs and over her cast, finally dropping them to the floor.

Deirdre experienced a resurgence of anxiety when he sat back and looked at her, but his gaze was filled with such reverence that those fears receded once again. The hand he skimmed up her leg was worshipful, and when he reached the nest of pale hair at the juncture of her thighs, he touched her with care that bordered on awe.

She felt totally exposed, yet treasured. Looking at Neil, seeing the way his large frame quivered with restrained desire, she marveled that fate had brought him to her.

"Neil . . . please . . ." she begged in a shaky whisper. "I want you."

He needed no more urging. Sitting back, he unsnapped his jeans and thrust them down his legs along with his briefs. Within seconds he was sliding over her, finding a place for himself between her thighs, threading his fingers through hers and anchoring them by her shoulders.

Bearing his weight on his elbows, he rubbed his hot body back and forth over hers. He made no attempt to penetrate her, simply sought the pleasure of his new level of touching. But the pleasure was galvanic, causing them both to breathe quickly and unevenly.

Deirdre had never before known such anticipation. She wasn't thinking about her fears, wasn't thinking about what would happen if Neil didn't find her lovemaking adequate. She was only thinking of the burning deep within her, knowing that she needed his possession now.

Eyes closed, she arched upward, hips straining toward his in a silent plea that dashed the last of his resistance. Nudging her legs farther apart, he positioned himself, then tightened his fingers around hers.

"Look at me, Deirdre," he whispered. "Look at me, babe."

Her eyes opened, then grew wider when, ever so slowly, he entered her. She felt him clearly, sliding deeper and deeper; it was as though each individual cell inside her responded to his presence, transmitting one heady message after another to her brain. By the time he filled her completely, she knew that she'd never, never be the same again.

Neil closed his eyes and let out a long and tremulous sigh. Satisfaction was so clearly etched on his features that Deirdre would have breathed a sigh of relief, too, had she been able to. But he'd begun to move inside her, and breathing became increasingly difficult. All she could do was to give herself up to the spiral of passion he created.

The heat built steadily. Neil set a pace that maximized her pleasure, knowing precisely when to slow, precisely when to speed up. She moved to his rhythm, following his lead with a flair of her own that drove him on and up.

Then, when the fire within her became too hot for containment, she arched her back a final time, caught a sudden deep breath and dissolved into a seemingly endless series of spasms. Somewhere in the middle, Neil joined her, holding himself at the very entrance of her womb while his body pulsed and quivered.

It was a long time before either of them could speak, a long time during which the only sounds in the room were the harsh gasping for air and the softer, more gentle patter of the rain. Only when they'd begun to breath more normally did Neil slide to the side, but he brought her with him, settling them face to face on the pillow.

"Well," he asked softly, "what do you think?"

For an instant, Deirdre's old fears crowded in on her. "What do *you* think?" she whispered.

"I think," he said slowly, reining in a smug smile, "that for a lady with a sharp tongue and a questionable disposition, you're one hell of a lover."

7

RELIEF WASHED OVER HER, this time thoroughly wiping away whatever lingering doubts she'd had. A smile lit her face, unwaveringly, even as she raised her voice in mock protest.

"Sharp tongue? Questionable disposition? It was all because of you, Neil Hersey. You were the one who wasn't supposed to be here!"

Neil was undaunted. His own euphoria was too great. "And if I hadn't been," he ventured naughtily, "just think of all we'd have missed."

Deirdre had no suitable answer for that, so she simply continued to smile, and he was content to bask in her sunshine. After a time, he tenderly brushed a damp wisp of hair from her cheek.

"You're looking happy."

"I am . . . happy . . . satisfied . . . relieved."

"Was it that awful—the thought of our making love?" he chided.

"Oh, no, Neil," she answered quickly. "It was exciting. But you knew I was frightened."

"I'm still not sure why. It couldn't have been the athletic thing alone. Did it have something to do with the fellow who burned you once?"

She thought about that. "Indirectly, I suppose." Her gaze dropped. "Things were okay between us . . . sexually. It's just that when he got the urge to leave, he up and left, like there really wasn't anything worth sticking around for. On a subconscious level, I may have taken it more personally than I should have." She lapsed into silence as she considered why that had been. Her fingers moved lightly over the hair on Neil's chest in a reminder of what had just passed between them, and it gave her the courage to go on.

"I think it relates more to my family than Seth. I've always been the black sheep, the one who didn't fit in. My mother is the epitome of good manners, good looks and feminine poise. My sister takes after her. I've always been different, and they've made no secret of their opinion of me."

He cupped her throat in the vee of his hand, while his thumb drew circles on her collarbone. "They don't think you're feminine enough?"

"No."

His laugh was a cocky one. "Shows how much they know."

She rewarded him with a shy smile. "You're talking sex, which is only one part of it, but you're good for my ego, anyway."

"And you're good for mine. I don't think I've ever had a woman want me as much as you did just now. I know damn well that sex was the last thing on your mind when you got here, and that makes your desire so precious. I'd like to think it wasn't just any man who could turn you on like that."

"It wasn't!" she exclaimed, then lowered her voice. "There's only been one man, and that was Seth. I'm not very experienced."

"Experienced women are a dime a dozen. You're worth far more."

"I've never been driven by sexual need. I've never seen myself as a sexual being."

"We're all sexual beings."

"To one degree or another, but those degrees can vary widely." She moved her thigh between his, finding pleasure in the textural contrast of their bodies. "I guess what I'm saying is that I've always assumed myself to be at the lower end of the scale."

"Do you still?" he asked softly.

The look she gave him was every bit as soft. "With you? No."

He ran his hand down her spine, covered her bottom and pressed her hips intimately close. "That's good," he said, and sucked in a loud breath. "Because I think I'm needing you again."

Deirdre couldn't have been more delighted. Not only was he proving once again that her fears had been unfounded, but he was mirroring the state of her own reawakening desire. She followed the progress of her hand as it inched its way down his chest. "I think the needing is mutual."

"Any regrets?" he asked thickly.

"Only that I can't wrap both legs around you."

"It is a challenge with your cast. I didn't hurt you before, did I?"

She was fascinated by the whorl of hair around his navel. "Did I sound like I was in pain?" she asked distractedly.

"Dire pain."

"It had nothing to do with my leg." Her hand crept lower, tangling in the dark curls above his sex.

"Deirdre?" He was having trouble breathing again.

She was too engrossed in her exploration to take pity on him. "You have a beautiful body," she whispered. Her fingers grazed his tumescence. "I didn't have time to touch you before."

"Oh, God," he breathed when she took him fully into her grasp. His hand tightened on her shoulder, and he pressed his lips to her forehead. "Oh . . ."

"Do you like that?" she asked, cautiously stroking him.

"Oh, yes . . . harder . . . you can do it harder." His body was straining for her touch; when she strengthened it, he gave a moan of ecstasy. "Almost heaven—that's what it is."

"Almost?"

He opened his eyes and gazed at her then. "True heaven is when I'm inside." Inserting his leg between hers, he brought her thigh even higher. "You're hot and moist and tight, so tight. The way I slip in—" he put action to words "—shows how perfectly you . . . ummmmmm . . . how perfectly you were made . . . for me."

It was Deirdre's turn to gasp, then moan. He was lodged deeply within her, while his hand was caressing the rest of her with consummate expertise. When he withdrew, then surged back, she thought she'd explode.

The explosion wasn't long in coming. His mouth covered hers and he filled her with his tongue, as his manhood already filled her. One bold thrust echoed the other in a rhythm that repeated itself until all rhythm was suspended in a climactic surge.

This time when they tumbled back from that pyrotechnic plane, they had neither the strength nor the need to talk. Fitting Deirdre snugly into the curve of his body, Neil held her until her breathing was long and even. Soon after, he, too, was asleep.

THE NEXT DAY was the most glorious one Deirdre had ever known. She awoke in Neil's arms with a smile on her face, and if the smile ever faded, it was never for long. He instructed her to stay in bed while he showered, then he returned and carried her in for a bath. By the time he'd washed her to his satisfaction, they were both in need of satisfaction of another sort. So he carried her back to bed, where he proceeded to adore every bare inch of her body.

He taught her things about herself she'd never known, banishing any modesty she might have had and reaping the benefits. With deft fingers, an agile tongue and pulsing sex, he brought her to climax after climax, until she pleaded for mercy.

"A sex fiend!" she cried. "I'm stranded on an island with a sex fiend!"

"Look who's talking!" was all he had to say. Not only had she been as hungry as he, but she'd taken every one of the liberties with his body that he had with hers.

They didn't bother to get dressed that day. It seemed a waste of time and effort. The weather was as ominous as the thought of putting clothing between them. When they left the bedroom, they shared Deirdre's pajamas—the top was hers, the bottom his. He teased her, claiming that she'd brought along men's pajamas with precisely that goal in mind, but he wasn't about to complain when he knew all he had to do—whether in the kitchen, the living room or the den—was to raise her top, lower his bottom, and enter her with a fluid thrust.

Deirdre let his presence fill her, both body and mind. She knew they were living a dream, that reality lurked just beyond, waiting to pounce. But she refused to be distracted by other, more somber thoughts when she was feeling so complete. Neil accepted her. He'd seen her at her worst, yet he accepted her. His attraction to her wasn't based on who she was, what she did for a living, or what she wore; he liked her as the person she was.

Neil was similarly content. The realization that he was avoiding reality did nothing to temper his feelings about Deirdre. He refused to dwell on the fact that she didn't know about the downturn his life in Hartford had taken, because it didn't seem to matter. She was happy; he'd made her happy. She didn't care about his financial prospects or his reputation. She was satisfied to accept him as he was.

And so they didn't think about the future. One day melded into the next, each filled with relaxation, leisure activity, lovemaking. Deirdre finished one book and started a second. She got the hang of knitting well enough to begin work on the actual sweater, and made commendable headway on it. She exercised each day but made no attempt to devise new routines, loath to do something that might start her brooding on whether she'd be able to teach again.

Neil did his share of reading. He continued to take responsibility for most of the household chores, and it was his pleasure to do so. From time to time Deirdre tried to help, but he saw the frustration she suffered with her cast, and it was enough to tell him that he wasn't being used.

The bickering they'd done during those first three days was, for all intents and purposes, over. This was not to say that they agreed on everything, but compromise became the mode. Neil accepted the loud beat of Deirdre's music, while she accepted the drone of his radio-transmitted Celtics games. She subjected herself to a clobbering at Trivial Pursuit, while he endured the gyrations in *Saturday Night Fever*.

One night, when he was feeling particularly buoyant, he took a Havana cigar from his bag, lit it and sat back on the sofa in bliss. Deirdre, who'd watched in horror his elaborate ceremony of nipping off the end of the cigar, then moistening the tip, simply sat with one finger unobtrusively blocking her nose. It was an example of how far they'd come; as disgusting as she found the smell, she wasn't about to dampen his obvious pleasure.

He'd been smoking for several minutes before he cast her a glance and saw her pose. "Uh-oh. Bad?"

She shrugged. "Are't dose tings illegal in dis country?" she asked, careful to breathe through her mouth.

"It's illegal to import them. But if a foreigner brings them in for his own personal use and shares them with his friends, it's okay."

"Is dat how you got it?"

"I have a client from Jordan who has business interests here. He gave me a box several months ago." Neil eyed the long cigar with reverence. "I'm not usually a smoker, but I have to admit that if you want to smoke a cigar, this is the way to go."

"Da Mercedes of cigars?"

"Yup." Eyes slitted in pleasure, he put the cigar to his mouth, drew on it, then blew out a narrow stream of thick smoke. "Should I put it out?"

"Dot on my accou't. But do't ask me to kiss you later, commie breath."

His lips quirked at the corners. Leaning forward, he carefully placed the cigar in an ashtray, then stood and advanced on her.

She held up a hand. "Do't come closer. I dow what you're goi'g to do."

He propped his hands on the arm of her chair and bent so that his face was inches from hers. He was grinning. "I'll kiss you if I want to, and you'll like it, commie breath and all."

"Deil, I'm warding you—"

Her warning was cut short by his mouth, which took hers in a way that was at once familiar and new. After the initial capture, his lips softened and grew persuasive, coaxing hers into a response she was helpless to withhold.

When at last he ended the kiss, he murmured softly, "You can breathe now."

Deirdre's eyes were closed, and the hand that had protected her nose had long since abandoned that post and moved from the rich texture of his beard up into his thick, brown hair. "How can I do that...when you take my breath away...." When she pulled him back to her, he was more than willing to accede to her demands.

As time passed the cigar burned itself out, but neither of them noticed.

EARLY IN THE MORNING of their one-week anniversary on the island, Thomas called them from shore. Neil was the one to talk to him, but Deirdre, standing by, heard every word.

"How're you folks making out?"

Neil grinned, but made sure his voice was suitably sober. "Okay."

"I got your messages, but I've been away most of the week. I figured that you'd keep trying if there was any kind of emergency."

"He feels guilty," Deirdre whispered mischievously. "Serves him right."

Neil collared her with a playful arm as he spoke grimly back into the receiver. "We'll live."

"Deirdre's doing all right with that leg of hers?"

Neil hesitated before answering. Meanwhile, he toyed gently with Deirdre's earlobe. "The house has taken a beating. She's not very good with her crutches."

Deirdre kicked at his shin with her cast. He side-stepped her deftly.

"Oh," Thomas said. "Well, that's Victoria's problem. Are you two getting along?"

"Getting along?" Deirdre whispered. She slid her hand over Neil's ribs and tucked her fingers in the waistband of his jeans.

Neil cleared his throat and pulled a straight face. "We're still alive."

"You'll drive him crazy," she whispered. "He's dying of curiosity."

"Let him die," Neil whispered back, eyes dancing.

During the brief interlude, Thomas had apparently decided that what was happening between Neil and Deirdre was Victoria's problem, too. "Well," came his staticky voice, "I just wanted to let you know that you've got a store of fresh supplies on the dock."

"On the dock?" Neil looked at his watch. It was barely nine. "You must have been up before dawn."

"I left them last night."

"Coward."

"What's that?" came the static. "I didn't get that last word?"

Deirdre snickered noisily. Neil clamped a hand on her mouth. "I said, thank you," he yelled more loudly than necessary into the handset.

"Oh. Okay. I'll be out next week to pick you up, then. If there's any change in plans, give me a call."

For the first time, Neil's hesitation was legitimate. Looking down, he saw that Deirdre's too, was suddenly more serious. His fingers grew tighter on the handset.

"Will do" was all he said before switching off the instrument and replacing it on its stand. He stood silent for a minute with his arm still around Deirdre. Then, with a squeeze of her shoulder, he took a fast breath. "Hey, do you see what I see?"

She was ready for a diversion. Any diversion. Thomas's last comment had been a depressant. "I don't know. What do you see?"

He raised his eyes to the window. "The sun. Well, maybe not the sun itself, but it's brighter out there than it's been in a week, and it hasn't rained since yesterday, which means that the paths will have begun to dry out, which means that I can get the things in from the dock pretty quick, which means—" he gave her shoulder another squeeze "—that we can take a walk."

Deirdre followed his gaze, then looked back up at him. "I'd like that," she said softly. "I'd like it a lot."

THE BREAK IN THE WEATHER offered new realms of adventure for them. As though determined to restake its claim after a long absence, the sun grew stronger from one day to the next. The air remained cool, and Deirdre's mobility was limited by her crutches, but she and Neil managed to explore most of the small island. When they weren't wandering in one direction or another, they were perched atop high boulders overlooking the sea. They watched the sun rise one morning, watched the sun set one evening, and in between they agreed that neither of them had ever visited as serene a place.

Unfortunately, with greater frequency as the days passed, their serenity was disturbed by the memory of Thomas's parting words. He'd be by to pick them up at the end of a week, and that week seemed far too short. Deirdre began to brood more and more about Providence, Neil about Hartford, and though the making up was always breathtaking, they began to bicker again.

Finally, three days before they were to leave, things came to a head. They'd finished dinner and were seated side by side in the den, ostensibly watching *Raiders of the Lost Ark*, but in truth paying it little heed. With an abruptness that mirrored his mood, Neil switched off the set.

Deirdre shot him a scowl. She'd been thinking about leaving the island, and the prospect left her cold. "What did you do that for?"

"You're picking your fingernail again. The sound drives me crazy!" What really drove him crazy was the thought of returning to Hartford, but Deirdre's nail picking was as good a scapegoat as any.

"But I wanted to watch the movie."

"How can you watch the movie when you're totally engrossed in your nail?"

"Maybe if you weren't rubbing that damned beard of yours, I'd be able to concentrate."

His eyes darkened. "You haven't complained about my beard for days." In fact, she'd complimented him on it. It was filling in well, she'd said, and looked good. He'd agreed with her assessment. "And maybe I'm rubbing it to drown out the sound of your picking! Why do you *do* that?"

"It's a nervous habit, Neil. I can't help it."

"So why are you nervous? I thought you were supposed to be calm and relaxed."

"I am!" she cried, then, hearing herself, dropped both her gaze and her voice. "I'm not."

Silence hung in the air between them. When Deirdre looked up at last, she found Neil studying her with a pained expression on his face.

"We have to talk," he said quietly.

"I know."

"Thomas will be here soon."

"I know."

"You'll go back to Providence. I'll go back to Hartford."

"I *know*."

"So what are we going to do about it?"

She shrugged, then slanted him a pleading glance. "Tell him we're staying for another week?" Even more frightening to her than the prospect of returning to Providence was the prospect of leaving Neil.

He snorted and pushed himself from the sofa, pacing to the far side of the room before turning on his heel. "I can't do that, Deirdre. Much as I wish it, I can't."

"Then what do you suggest?"

He stood with one hand on his hip, the other rubbing the back of his neck. His gaze was unfocused, alternately shifting from the wall to the floor and back. "I don't know, damn it. I've been trying to think of solutions—No, that's wrong. I've avoided thinking about going back since I arrived, and as a result, I have no solutions. Then there's *this* complication."

Deirdre didn't like the sound of his voice. "What complication?"

He looked her in the eye. "Us."

It was like a blow to her stomach. Though she knew he was right, she couldn't bear to think of what they'd shared in negative terms. "Look," she argued, holding up a hand in immediate self-defense. "*We* don't have to be a complication. You can go your way, I can go mine. *Fini.*"

"Is that how you want it?"

"No."

"How do you want it?"

"I don't know," she cried in frustration. "You're not the only one who's avoided thinking about going back. I haven't found any more solutions than you have."

"But we do agree that we want to keep on seeing each other."

"Yes!"

His shoulders sagged in defeat. "Then it is a complication, Deirdre. On top of everything else, what we have is very definitely a complication." He turned to stare out the window.

Deirdre, in turn, stared at him. "Okay, Neil," she began softly. "You're right. We have to talk. About everything." When he didn't move, she continued.

"When we first came here, you were as bad-tempered as I was. I know my reasons, but I've never really known yours. At first I didn't want to know, because I have enough problems of my own. Then, when things got . . . better between us, I didn't want to ask for fear of upsetting the apple cart." She was sitting forward on the couch, a hand spread palm down on each thigh. "But I'm asking now. If we're going to figure anything out, I have to know. What happened, Neil? What happened in Hartford that brought you up here in such a temper? Why did you need to escape?"

Neil dropped his chin to his chest, her questions echoing in his brain. The moment of truth had come. He gnawed on the inside of his cheek, as though even doing something so pointless would be an excuse for not answering. But it wasn't. Deirdre was curious, and intelligent. As much as he wished he didn't have to tell her, she more than anyone deserved to know.

He turned to face her but made no move to close the distance between them. "I have," he said with a resigned sigh, "a major problem back home. It involves one of my principal clients—strike that, one of my prinicipal *ex*-clients, a very large corporation based in Hartford." He hesitated.

"Go on," she urged softly. "I'm with you."

"I've been chief counsel for the corporation for three years, and during that time I've come to be increasingly familiar with various aspects of the business. Last summer, quite inadvertently, I stumbled onto a corruption scheme involving the president of the corporation."

Deirdre held her breath and watched him with growing apprehension. She refused to believe that he'd knowingly condone corruption, yet, as corporate counsel, his job was to side with his client.

"No," he said, reading her fear, "I didn't demand a cut—"

"I never thought you would! But you must have been put in an awful position."

He was relieved by her obvious sincerity, but in some ways that made his task all the more difficult. He would have liked to be able to tell her that his practice was successful and growing even more so. He would have liked to have shone in her eyes. But the facts were against him.

Deirdre didn't deserve this. Hell, *he* didn't deserve it!

"Awful is putting it mildly," he declared. "I could have chosen to look the other way, but it went against every principle I'd ever held. So I took the matter before the board of directors. That was when things fell apart."

"What do you mean?"

"They were involved! All of them! They knew exactly what was going on, and their only regret was that I'd found out!"

Deirdre felt her anger rising on his behalf. "What did you do?"

"I resigned. I had no other choice. There was no way I'd sit back and watch them pad their own pockets at the expense of not only their stockholders but their employees. Their employees! The last people who could afford to be gypped!"

"But I don't understand, Neil. If you resigned, isn't it all over? You may have lost one client, but you have others, don't you?"

"Oh, yes," he ground out with more than a little sarcasm. "But those others have dwindled with a suddenness that can't possibly be coincidental." His jaw was tight. "It seems that Wittnauer-Douglass wasn't satisfied simply with my resignation. The executive board wanted to make sure I wouldn't do anything to rock a very lucrative boat."

She was appalled. "They blackballed you."

"Worse. They passed word around that I'd been the mastermind behind the corruption scheme. According to the chairman of the board—and I got this from a reliable source—if I hadn't left, they'd have leveled charges against me."

"But they can't say that!"

"They can say anything they damn well please!"

"Then they can't *do* it!"

"I'm not so sure. There's a helluva lot of murky paperwork in the archives of any large corporation. That paperwork can be easily doctored if the right people give the go-ahead."

"But why would the board at Wittnauer-Douglass want to even mention corruption? Wouldn't it spoil their own scheme?"

"Not by a long shot. They simply reorganize, shift outlets, juggle a few more documents. When you've got power, you've got power. It's as simple as that."

"And you can't fight them." It was a statement, a straight follow-up to Neil's. Unfortunately it touched a nerve in him that was all too raw.

"What in the hell can I do?" he exploded, every muscle in his body rigid. "They've spread word so far and so fast that it's become virtually impossible for me to practice law in Hartford! The major corporations won't touch me. The medium-sized ones are leery. And it's gone way beyond my profession. Nancy—the woman I was seeing—quickly opted out, which was okay, because it was only a matter of time before we'd have split, anyway. But before I knew what had happened, I'd been replaced as chairman of the hospital fund-raising drive. That did hurt. Word is that I'm a crook, and even if some people believe in my innocence, there are still appearances to uphold. Hell, I can't even find a squash partner these days. I've become a regular pariah!"

"They can't do that!"

"They've done it," he lashed back. His anger was compounding itself, taking on even greater force than it had held in Hartford, mainly because he detested having to dump this on Deirdre. "I've worked my tail off to build a successful practice, and they've swept it away without a care in the world. And do you know what the worst part is?" He was livid now, furious with himself. "I didn't see it coming! I was naive . . . stupid!"

Deirdre was on her feet, limping toward him. "It wasn't your fault—"

He interrupted, barely hearing her argument over the internal din of his self-reproach. "How could I have possibly spent so much time working with those people and not have seen them for what they are? I'm too trusting! I've always been too trusting! Good guys finish last, isn't that what they say? Well, it's true!"

She took his arm. "But trusting is a good way to be, Neil," she argued with quiet force. "The alternative is to be an eternal skeptic, or worse, paranoid, and you couldn't live that way."

"My friends. They even got to my *friends*."

"A real friend wouldn't be gotten to."

"Then I've been a poor judge of character on that score, too."

"You're being too harsh on yourself—"

"And it's about time! Someone should have kicked me in the pants years ago. Maybe if they had, I wouldn't have been such a damned optimist. Maybe I would have seen all this coming. Maybe I wouldn't be in such a completely untenable position now."

"You can find new clients," she ventured cautiously.

"Not the kind I want. My expertise is in dealing with large corporations, and those won't come near me now."

"Maybe not in Hartford—"

"Which means relocating. Damn it, I don't want to relocate. At least, not for that reason."

"But things aren't hopeless, Neil. You have a profession that you're skilled in—"

"And look where it's gotten me," he seethed. "I have a great office, two capable associates and a steadily diminishing clientele. I have a condominium, which the people I once called friends won't deign to visit. I have a record for charity work that's come to a dead halt. I have squash gear and no partner."

Deirdre dropped her hand from his stiff arm. "You also think you have a monopoly on self-pity. Well, you don't, Neil. You're not the only one who has problems. You're not the only one who's frustrated."

"Frustrated?" He raked rigid fingers through his hair. "Now *that's* the understatement of the year. And while we're at it, you can add guilt to the list of my transgressions. I came up here and took every one of those frustrations out on you!"

"But you weren't the only one to do it! I used you for that too, Neil, so I'm as guilty as you are."

"Yeah." His voice was calm now. "Only difference is that your problem has a solution in sight. Once the cast is off—"

"It's not only my leg," Deirdre snapped, turning away from him. "I wouldn't have been in such a lousy mood if it was simply a question of my leg. There's a whole other story to my life, and if you think that in its own way my situation isn't as frustrating as yours, you can add egotistical to that list you're drawing up."

There was silence behind her. For the first time since he'd begun his tirade, Neil's thoughts took a tangent. *A whole other story to my life,* she'd said. He was suddenly more nervous than he'd been angry moments before, inexplicably fearful that his world was about to collapse completely.

"What is it—that other story?"

Head down, she hobbled over to rest her hip against the desk. A dry laugh slipped from her throat. "It's ironic. There you are, without a corporation to represent. Here I am, with a corporation I don't want."

"What are you talking about?"

Slowly she raised her head. Almost reluctantly she replied, "Joyce Enterprises. Have you ever heard of it?"

"I've heard of it. It's based in . . ." The light dawned. "Providence. You're that Joyce? It's yours?"

"Actually, my family's. My father died six months ago, and my sister took over the helm."

Neil frowned. "I didn't make the connection . . . I never . . . it doesn't fit."

"With who I am?" She smiled sadly. "You're right. It doesn't fit. I don't fit, and that's the problem. My parents always intended that the business stay in the family. Sandra—my sister—just can't handle it. I have two uncles who are involved, but they're as ill-equipped to run things as my mother is."

Neil had come to stand before her. "So they want you in."

"Right."

"But you don't want in."

"Right again. I tried it once and hated it. I'm just not the type to dress up all day and entertain, which is largely what the head of a business like that has to do. I don't take to diplomatic small talk, and I don't take to being a pretty little thing on display."

"That I can believe," he quipped.

Deirdre responded to his teasing with a scowl. "I wish my family could believe it, but they won't. They keep insisting that I'm their only hope, and maybe I would be able to handle the management end of the business, but the political end would drive me up a tree! For six months now they've been after me, and while I was busy doing my own thing I had an excuse. At least, it was one I could grasp at. I've always known that sooner or later, as I got older, I'd slow down, but I thought I had time to find a substitute. Now I don't. Suddenly I can't do my own thing, and they've started hounding me to do theirs. Even before I left the hospital they were on me." She paused for a breath, then continued.

"They think I'm selfish, and maybe I am, because I want to be happy, and I know I won't be if I'm forced to be involved in the business. It's really a joke—their pushing me this way. I've always been odd in their minds. I'm a failure. They look down their noses at the work I do. And even beyond that, I don't have a husband, or children, which compounds my sin. What good am I? Nothing I do is right, so they say. Yet they stand over me and insist that I help run Joyce." She rubbed a throbbing spot on her forehead, then looked up at Neil.

"The family needs me. The business needs me. Can I stand by and let it all go down the tubes? Because it will, Neil. I keep telling them to bring in outside help, but they refuse, and if they continue to do that, the whole thing is doomed. Oh, it may take a while. The corporation is like a huge piece of machinery. It's showing signs of wear and tear right now, but the gears are still turning. When it comes time to oil them, though, and there's no one capable of doing the job, things will slow down, then eventually grind to a halt."

She gave a quick, little headshake, more of a shiver. "Talk of guilt, I've got it in spades. I have a *responsibility*, my mother keeps reminding me. And that's the worst part, because as much as I can't bear the thought of having anything to do with the business, I do feel the responsibility. I deny it to them. I've denied it to myself. But it's there." She looked down at her fingers and repeated more softly, "It's there."

Neil wrapped his hand around her neck and kneaded it gently. "We're a fine twosome, you and I. Between us, we've got a pack of ills and no medicine."

She gave a meek laugh. "Maybe the island drugstore has something?"

He sighed. "The island drugstore filled the prescription for two souls who needed a break, but I'm afraid it doesn't have anything for curing the ills back home."

"So," she breathed, discouraged. "We're back where we started. What are we going to do?"

He looked at her intently, then dipped his head and took her lips with a sweetness that wrenched at her heart. "We are going to spend the next three days enjoying each other. That is, if you don't mind dallying with a man who has a very dubious future ..."

It was at that moment, with Neil standing close, looking at her as though her answer were more important to him than anything else in the world, that Deirdre knew she loved him.

She smiled softly. "If you don't mind dallying with a woman who would rather spend the rest of her life on this island than go back to the mainland and face up to her responsibilities ..."

His answer was a broad smile and another kiss, this one deeper and more soul reaching than anything that had come before. It was followed by a third, then a fourth, and before long, neither Neil nor Deirdre could think of the future.

THEIR FINAL DAYS on the island were spent much as the preceding ones had been, though now there was direction to their thoughts, rather than a random moodiness. For his part, Neil was relieved to have told Deirdre everything, even if the telling hadn't solved a thing. She'd accepted his quandary without criticism, and her affection—yes, he was sure it was that—for him seemed, if anything, to have deepened.

For her part, Deirdre was relieved to have shared her burden with an understanding soul. Neil hadn't jumped on her for her failings; if anything, his affection—yes she was sure it was that—for her seemed stronger than ever.

If that affection took on a frantic quality at times, each attributed it to the fact that the clock was running out.

Thomas had arranged to pick them up at eight o'clock in the morning on that last day. So the night before they found themselves cleaning the house, making sure that everything was as it had been when they'd arrived two weeks before. Tension suddenly surrounded them, reducing them to nearly the same testy state they'd been in when they'd arrived.

Neil did a final round of laundry, inadvertently tossing Deirdre's teal green sweatshirt into the wash with the towels, half of which were an electric blue not far different from her sweatshirt, half of which were pure white. When the white towels emerged with a distinct green tinge, he swore loudly.

"Goddamn it! I thought you'd packed this thing already!"

"I haven't packed anything yet." She'd been putting that particular chore off for as long as possible. Now, studying the once-white towels, she scowled. "Didn't you see the sweatshirt when you put the towels in?"

"How could I see it in with these blue ones?"

"The sweatshirt's green!"

"That's close enough."

"You must be color-blind."

"I am not color-blind."

They were glaring at each other over the washing machine. Deirdre was the first to look away. "Okay," she said, sighing. "We can put the white towels through again, this time with bleach."

"The little tag says not to use bleach."

Fiery eyes met his. "I've used bleach on towels before, and it does the trick. If you don't want to take the risk, you find a solution." Turning, she swung back to her cleaning of the refrigerator, leaving Neil to grudgingly add bleach to a second load.

Not long after, intent on doing the packing she'd put off, Deirdre was headed for the bedroom, when her crutch caught on the edge of the area rug in the living room. She stumbled and fell, crying out in annoyance as well as surprise.

"Who put that stupid rug there?" she screamed.

Neil was quickly by her side, his voice tense. "That 'stupid' rug has been in exactly the same spot since we got here. Weren't you watching where you were going?"

"It's the damned rubber tips on these crutches!" She kicked at them with her good foot. "They catch on everything!"

Rescuing the crutches, he put an arm across her back and helped her up. "They haven't bothered you before. Are you okay?"

"I'm fine," she snarled, rubbing her hip.

"Then you're lucky. Damn it, Deirdre, are you trying to kill yourself? Why don't you watch where you're going next time?"

"Watch where I'm going? I was watching!"

"Then you were going too fast!"

"I wasn't going any faster than I ever go!"

"Which is too fast!"

Deirdre, who had returned the crutches to their rightful place, backed away from him, incensed. "I don't need advice from you! I've taken care of myself for years, and I'll do it again! Just because you've helped me out this week doesn't give you the right to order me around. If you really wanted to help me, you'd offer to take that damned corporation off my back!"

"If you really wanted to help *me*, you'd *give* me the damned corporation!" he roared back.

For long minutes they stood glaring at each other. Both pairs of eyes flashed; both pairs of nostrils flared. Gradually both chests stopped heaving, and their anger dissipated.

"It's yours," Deirdre said quietly, her eyes glued to his.

"I'll take it," he countered, but his voice, too, was quiet.

"It's a bizarre idea."

"Totally off the wall."

"But it could offer an out for both of us."

"That's right."

They stood where they were for another long minute. Then, resting a hand lightly on her back, Neil urged her toward the sofa. When they were both seated, he crossed one leg over his knee, propped his elbow on the arm of the sofa and chafed his lower lip with his thumb.

"I've done a lot of thinking since we talked the other night," he began, hesitating at first, then gaining momentum. "I've been over and over the problem, trying to decide what I want to do. There are times when I get angry, when the only thing that makes any sense to me is revenge. Then the anger fades, and I realize how absurd that is. It's also self-defeating, when what I really want to do is to practice law." He paused, lowered his hand to his lap and looked at her. "You have a corporation that you don't want. I could make good use of it."

Nervously she searched his features. "For revenge?"

"No. Maybe it'd be a sort of reprisal, but that wouldn't be my main objective. I need something, Deirdre. It kills me to have to say that, especially to you. It's hard for a man—for anyone, I suppose—to admit that he's short on options. But I'm trying to face facts, and the sole fact in this case is that Hartford is no longer a viable place for me to work."

"You said you didn't want to relocate."

"I said I didn't want to relocate because of Wittnauer-Douglass. Maybe it's convoluted logic, but I'm beginning to think that Joyce Enterprises would have attracted me regardless of the problems in Hartford. No matter what you see happening now within the company, Joyce has a solid reputation. I wouldn't be afraid to put my stock in it. And it may be the highest form of conceit, but I do think that I have something to offer. I'm a good lawyer. I'm intimately familiar with the workings of large corporations. I may not be an entrepreneur, but I know people who are. And I know of a headhunter who could help me find the best ones to work with.

"Unfortunately—" he took a breath and his eyes widened as he broached the next problem "—that would mean bringing in an outsider. From what you say, your family has been against that from the start, which raises the even more immediate issue of whether or not they'd even accept me."

Deirdre tipped up her chin in a gesture of defiance. "I hold an equal amount of stock to my mother and sister. If you were to enter the corporation alongside me, they wouldn't dare fight."

"But you don't want to enter the corporation. Wasn't that the point?"

"Yes, but if we were . . ." She faltered, struggling to find the least presumptive words. "If we were together. . . . I mean, if I made it clear that we were . . . involved . . ."

"That we were a steady couple, as in lovers?"

"Yes."

He gave his head a quick shake. "Not good enough. It'll have to be marriage."

"Marriage?" She'd wanted to think that they'd be tied somehow, but marriage was the ultimate in ties. "Isn't that a little radical?"

Neil shrugged, but nonchalance was the last thing he felt. He'd been searching for a way to bind Deirdre to him. He loved her. Somewhere along the line that realization had dawned, and it had fit him so comfortably that he hadn't thought of questioning it. He couldn't say the words yet; he felt too vulnerable. Marriage might be sudden, but it served his purposes well. "Radical only in that we've known each other for such a short time. We get along, don't we?"

"We fight constantly!" she argued, playing the devil's advocate. If she knew that Neil loved her she wouldn't have had an argument in the world. But he hadn't said those words, and she didn't have the courage to lay herself bare by saying them herself, so she felt obligated to resist.

"Not constantly. Only when we're frustrated by problems that seem beyond our control. We've had our smooth times, haven't we?"

"Yes," she admitted, albeit reluctantly.

"And if this whole plan solves our problems, we won't have cause to fight, will we?"

"Every married couple fights."

"Then we wouldn't be any different. Look at it objectively, Deirdre. We have similar values and interests. We've already proved that we can live with each other. If we survived these past two weeks, being together twenty-four hours a day, we've got one foot up on many other couples who marry."

She didn't want to look at it objectively. Love wasn't objective. "But we've known each other in such a limited sphere. This isn't the real world. It's possible that we could return to Providence and find that we *hate* each other."

"That's your insecurity talking."

"Okay, maybe it is. I don't think I'm cut out to be a corporate wife any more than I'm cut out to head that corporation." She waved a hand back and forth. "I'm not the prissy little hostess. I'm not the adorable little lady who always wears and says the right things."

"I'm not complaining about who you are. And I wouldn't ask you to do anything you're uncomfortable with. If we entertain—and I assume there'd be some of that—you'd look as beautiful as any woman in the room. And rather than having you cook we could take people out or have something catered."

"In my modest town house?" she squeaked.

"In the house I'd buy for us." He sat forward, determination strong in the gaze he sent her. "I'm not a gigolo, Deirdre. I wouldn't go into this if I felt I was getting a free ride. You may not know it yet, but I do have my pride. If we agree to go ahead with this scheme, I'll work my tail off in the business. I'll be the one to support us, and that means providing the kind of home for you that I think you deserve. I guess I'm old-fashioned in that way."

"Does that mean I can't work or do whatever else I want?"

"You can do anything you want. I'm not *that* old-fashioned. And if you think I'm bothered by the thought of your teaching aerobics, think again. I adore your athletic body. Don't you know that by now?"

She simply slanted him a wry glance.

"Exercise is the way to go nowadays," he continued. "I'll be proud to have a wife who keeps her body toned."

"If I can," she muttered. "Whether I teach or not is still a big question."

"You'll teach. I told you that. When the cast comes off, you'll have physical therapy or whatever else it takes to get that leg working right."

"But...even if that happens, many of my classes are evening ones. How will you feel when you come home to an empty house after a hard day's work and there isn't even a hot meal ready?"

"I can cook. You know that. I'll be proud of you, Deirdre. My wife will be doing something that's constructive, something she enjoys." He paused for a breath, sobering. "And while we're talking of pride, if you agree to marry me, I'll insist on a prenuptial agreement."

Deirdre couldn't conceal a quick flare of hurt. "I don't want your money!"

"You've got it backside-to. It's you I want to protect. If you agree to marry me, I'll draw up a paper stating that your holdings in Joyce Enterprises—and anything else you now have to your name—will remain solely yours. If you should decide, at any point, that you want out of the marriage, you'll have everything you had when you entered into it. And if, at any point, you decide that I'm a detriment to Joyce Enterprises, you'll have the full right to can me."

She couldn't imagine that ever happening. For that matter, she couldn't imagine ever wanting out of a marriage to Neil. Unless he wanted it. "But what about your interests? They won't be protected if you sign a document like that. You thought you'd been naive regarding Wittnauer-Douglass. Isn't your plan now equally shortsighted?"

"I'd rather think of it as a challenge, one I'm approaching with my eyes wide open. I think I can make a go of running Joyce Enterprises, and if I do that, you won't have any cause to let me go. Like I said before, I'm not looking for a handout. I'm prepared to do the job. Yes, you'd be doing me a favor by giving me the chance, but I'd be doing you every bit as big a favor by relieving you of a responsibility you don't want."

He took her hand and studied the shape of her slender fingers. "You'd have a husband, which would please your family. And don't you think it's about time, anyway? I know it is for me. I'm not getting any younger. I'm more than ready to settle down."

But love? What about love? Deirdre pleaded silently. "Somehow it seems very... calculated."

"Sometimes the best things are."

"You don't have to marry me. We could still work all of this out."

"I'm sure we could, but marriage will be expedient when it comes to your family. They don't have to know about any agreement we sign. As far as they're concerned, what is yours is mine. I'll be a member of your family. The 'family business' will stay intact." He curved his fingers around hers and lowered his voice. "And I *want* to marry you. I wouldn't be suggesting it if that weren't the case."

But why do you want to marry me? she ached to ask, but didn't. He could give her the answer she craved, which would thrill her, or he could repeat the practical reasons he'd listed earlier, which would distress her. Rather than take the risk, she simply accepted his statement without prodding.

"Will you marry me, Deirdre?" he asked softly.

She met his gaze, knowing that love shone in her own with a strength she was helpless to dim. Silently she nodded, and closed her fingers around his.

8

AS HE'D PROMISED, Thomas was at the dock bright and early the next morning to pick them up. His curiosity was evident in the surreptitious glances he cast toward Deirdre, then Neil, at well-spaced intervals. They simply smiled at each other, feeling smug, but more than that, pleased with what lay ahead. If they'd dreaded the day they'd have to leave their island refuge, the knowledge that they were going to be together reduced that dread to a small twinge of sentimentality as the island faded behind them.

Neil had wanted to drive Deirdre back to Providence, but she insisted, with reason, he finally agreed, that it made no sense for her to leave her car in Maine when she'd want to use it at home. So he followed her on the highway, making sure she stopped periodically to stretch, then later, eat lunch.

It was mid-afternoon when they pulled up at Deirdre's mother's house. They'd discussed that, too, agreeing that the sooner they broke the news of their impending marriage to Maria Joyce the better. And, anticipating that the woman might give Deirdre a hard time, given her history of doing just that, Neil was vehement that he be present.

Maria was in the library when Deirdre called out from the front door. She came quickly, exclaiming loudly even before she entered the hall, "Deirdre! It's about time! I've been worried sick about where you were and how you were making out. If I hadn't thought to call Victoria—" She stopped short when she caught sight of her daughter, leaning on her crutches, beside a tall, bearded man in jeans. "Good Lord," she whispered, staring at the pair, "what have you brought home this time?"

Deirdre felt a movement by her elbow and knew that Neil was trying not to laugh. For that matter, so was she. In her eyes, Neil looked positively gorgeous, but she knew that her mother was wondering what the cat had dragged in.

"Mother, I'd like you to meet Neil Hersey. Neil, Maria Joyce."

Neil stepped forward and extended a firm hand, which Maria had no choice but to meet. "It's my pleasure, Mrs. Joyce. Deirdre has told me a lot about you."

Maria didn't take the time to wonder about the nature of that telling. She was too concerned about retrieving her hand from what was a far-too-confident grip. She nodded at Neil, but her focus was quickly on Deirdre.

"Victoria finally admitted that you'd gone to Maine. I can't believe you did that, Deirdre. The place is totally isolated, and in your condition—"

"My condition is fine. And Neil was there with me." Before her mother could pounce on that, she rushed on. "Neil is a friend of Victoria's, too. Now he's a friend of mine. Furthermore—" she looked at Neil "—we're going to be married. We wanted you to be the first to know." She took perverse delight in her mother's stunned expression.

For a minute the older woman was speechless. Then, pressing a hand to her heart, she revived.

"You can't be serious."

"We are. Very."

"Deirdre, you don't know this man!" She gave Neil a once-over that was disapproving at best.

"You'd be surprised, mother. Two weeks on an island, with no one else around—you can get to know a man pretty well."

Neil rolled his eyes at her smug tone and quickly sought to make amends to Maria. "What Deirdre means is that we had a chance to talk more than many people do in months. We shared responsibility for the house and everything to do with our daily lives. We feel that our marriage would be a good one."

Maria, who'd been eyeing him warily during his brief speech, closed her fingers around the single strand of pearls she was wearing with her very proper silk dress. "I think I need a drink," she said, and turned toward the living room.

Deirdre took off after her, with Neil following in her wake. "It's the middle of the afternoon! You don't need a drink in the middle of the afternoon!"

"Oh, yes, I do," came Maria's voice. She was already at the elegant cherrywood bar, fishing ice from a bucket. "When a woman hears that, after years of nagging, her daughter has decided on the spur of the moment to get married—and to a man she thinks she knows, but can't possibly, since she met him a mere two weeks ago—she needs a drink, *regardless* of the time of day!"

Deirdre took a deep breath and sent Neil a helpless glance before lowering herself to a nearby ottoman. "I think you ought to listen to the rest of what I have to tell you before you pass judgment. You may say something you'll later regret."

"I doubt that," Maria stated. She'd poured a healthy dose of bourbon into the glass and was standing stiffly by the bar. "I don't know where I failed with you, Deirdre, but I very definitely have failed. I've tried to instill in you certain values, and you've rejected every one of them. I tried to raise a lady, but you insist on running around in leotards—"

"Not leotards, mother. A tank top and running shorts. Leotards cut off my circulation."

She waved that aside. "Whatever. The point's the same. I tried to raise you with a sense of family, but you've insisted in going your own way. I've tried to make you see that you have an obligation to the business, but you won't hear of that. And now, when you've got nothing better to do with your time, instead of giving us a hand, you run off, meet up with a passing...hippie, and decide to marry him."

Neil, who'd been standing quietly at Deirdre's shoulder, felt that he'd heard enough. He didn't mind the insults to him, but they were a smaller part of insults to Deirdre, and he wouldn't have that. "I don't think you understand the situation, Mrs. Joyce," he said with such authority that Maria was forced to listen. "I am not a hippie, nor am I passing. If you've formed an opinion of me based on the way I look, I think you should remember that I've just come from a two-week vacation. The bulk of my life is spent in tailored suits, suits that would hold their own—" he looked at the bench before the grand piano "—with that Dunhill tapestry." He shifted his gaze to the small painting to the left of the bar. "Or that Modigliani." He dropped his eyes to the marble coffee table by Deirdre's knees. "Or that Baccarat vase."

Deirdre looked up at him. "I'm impressed," she mouthed.

He nudged her hip with his knee, shushing her with a frown.

Maria arched a well-shaped brow, but she wasn't about to be fully appeased. "The slickest of con men pick up a wealth of knowledge about fine accessories, Mr. Hersey. What is it you do for a living?"

"I'm a lawyer. I head my own firm in Hartford, specializing in corporate work. I can give you a full list of my credits, starting with law review at Harvard, but I don't think that's necessary. Suffice it to say that in recent years I've done work for Jennings and Lange, KronTech, and the Holder Foundation, as well as the Faulkner Company here in Providence." He was confident that the corporations he'd named would give him solid recommendations. He was equally confident that Maria Joyce had heard of them. She would have also heard of Wittnauer-Douglass. There was always the possibility that if the woman ran a check on him, she'd come across that problem, but it was a risk he'd have to take. And besides, by the time she learned anything, his marriage to Deirdre would be a fait accompli.

Maria dipped her head in reluctant acknowledgment of his credentials. "All right. I'll admit that my judgment may have been premature, but the fact remains that this marriage is very sudden. When was it going to take place?"

Deirdre opened her mouth, but Neil spoke first. "As soon as the law will allow. I believe there's a three-day waiting period once the license has been taken out and the blood tests done. I know a judge here in Providence who might cut even that down."

Maria studied her bourbon, pressing her lips together as she ingested that information. "Is there a rush?" She sent Deirdre a meaningful glance. "I know that there are home tests on the market that can give instant results—"

"I am not pregnant, mother," Deirdre interrupted. "And even if I were, I'd have thought you'd be pleased. You've been harping on having grandchildren since I was old enough to vote."

"Every woman wants grandchildren," Maria countered in self-defense.

"So you've said many times. And here's your chance. I don't know why you're complaining. Even if I *were* pregnant, Neil and I will be married before anyone is the wiser. At most, the baby would be born two weeks early, so to speak, which no one would think twice about. You wouldn't have any cause for embarrassment."

Maria scowled at her daughter. "All right," she said crossly. "Forget a pregnancy." Her annoyance broadened to include Neil. "You'll get married and take off for Hartford, leaving Joyce Enterprises in the lurch yet again. Honestly, Deirdre, is that fair?"

Neil answered. "We won't be living in Hartford. We'll be living here."

Maria arched a skeptical brow. "You'd walk away from that successful law practice?"

"I can practice law anywhere," he returned, tamping down a moment's discomfort. "Providence is as good a place as any."

"The fact is, Mother," Deirdre spoke up, "that we are going to bail you out, after all. Neil has agreed to help me with Joyce Enterprises."

For the second time in a very short period, Maria Joyce was speechless. She looked from Deirdre to Neil and back, then raised her glass and took a bolstering drink. By the time she'd lowered the glass, she'd regained a small measure of her composure, though not enough to keep the glass from shaking in her hand. She set it carefully on the bar.

"That," she began slowly, "is an unexpected turn."

"So is our wedding," Deirdre pointed out, "but it all makes sense. You've been after me for years to help with the business. I've been convinced that I'm not right for the job, but I'm equally convinced that Neil is." And she was. She had no doubts but that Neil could handle Joyce Enterprises. "You've wanted to keep things in the family. Neil will be in the family. What more could Dad have asked for than a son-in-law who could take over where his daughters left off?"

"But he's a lawyer," Maria argued, though more meekly this time. "He's not trained in this type of work."

"Neither am I—nor Sandra, for that matter."

Neil joined in. "I've worked closely with large corporations like Joyce for years, so I'm starting with a definite advantage. And I've had the benefit of seeing how other corporations function, which means that I can take the best of the systems and strategies I've seen and implement them at Joyce." He paused. "I think it could work out well for all of us, Mrs. Joyce. I assure you that I wouldn't be putting my career on the line if I didn't feel that the odds were in my favor."

Maria appeared to have run out of arguments. She raised both brows and nervously fingered her pearls. "I . . . it looks like you've thought things out."

"We have," Deirdre said.

The older woman shook her head, for the first time seeming almost confused. "I don't know, Deirdre. It's so sudden. . . . I was hoping that when my daughters got married they'd have big weddings, with lots of flowers and music and people."

Deirdre's shoulders rose with the deep breath she took. "I've never wanted that, Mother. I'll be perfectly happy with something small and private."

Maria looked at them both. "You will be happy? This is what you truly want?" They knew she wasn't referring to the wedding, but to the marriage itself.

Neil's hand met Deirdre's at her shoulder. "It is," Deirdre said softly.

Neil echoed the sentiment. "We'll be happy, Mrs. Joyce. You can take my word for it."

FEELING AS THOUGH they'd overcome their first hurdle, they left Maria, stopped for their marriage license and blood tests, then went to Deirdre's town house. Though Neil agreed that it was on the small side, he was charmed with the way she'd decorated it. Whereas old-world elegance had been the word at her mother's house, here everything was light and airy. The furniture was modern, low and cushiony. One room opened into another with barely a break. There were no Dunhill tapestries, no Modiglianis, no pieces of Baccarat crystal, but a small and carefully chosen selection of work by local artists and artisans.

"I feel very much at home here," Neil said to Deirdre as they lay in bed that night.

Chin propped on his chest, she smiled at him. "I'm glad."

"It's pretty and bright, uncluttered and unpretentious. Like you."

She tugged at his beard. "I think you want something. What is it?"

He smiled back and wrapped an arm around her waist. "Just that when we find the right home, you do it like this. I don't want to live in a museum or . . . or in a shrine to a decorator."

Deirdre narrowed her eyes. "Is that what your place is like?"

"A shrine to a decorator? Yes, it is, and I never thought twice about it until now, but I don't want that, Deirdre. There's a sophistication in the simplicity here. That's what I want. Okay?"

"Okay."

"No argument?"

"No argument."

"Good."

THEY HEADED for Hartford the next day. Neil had a long list of things to take care of, the most pressing and difficult of which was informing his associates that he'd be leaving. Both men were talented lawyers, but being young they hadn't yet developed reputations that would attract new business. Neil gave them the choice of joining other firms or taking over his practice themselves. When they opted for the latter, he assured them that he'd do everything he could to help them out, which included drawing up a letter to send his clients, telling them of the change and assuring them that they'd be in good hands if they remained with the firm.

The second order of business was putting his condominium on the market. The real estate agent, who had a list of people waiting for openings in that particular building, was delighted.

"Are you sure you want to sell it?" Deirdre asked timidly.

"Why not? I won't be living here."

"But if you find that you don't like Providence . . . or that things don't go well . . ."

He took her firmly by the shoulders. "I will like Providence, and things will go well. I'm making a commitment, Deirdre. There's no point in doing it halfway."

She didn't argue further, particularly since his confidence buoyed her. So they returned to Providence and went house hunting. Once again luck was on their side. They found a charming colonial on the outskirts of the city, not far from Deirdre's mother's house ironically, but in a younger neighborhood. The property encompassed three acres of land, with a wealth of trees and lush shrubbery, and though the house needed work, the previous owners had vacated several weeks before, and the work could begin immediately.

Three days after they arrived back from Maine, Deirdre and Neil were married in the church Deirdre had attended as a child. Her mother had made the arrangements—Deirdre felt it was as good a consolation prize as any—and there were more people, more flowers, more food than Deirdre might have chosen herself. But she was too happy that day to mind anything.

Neil looked breathtaking in his dark suit, white shirt, striped tie and cordovans. He'd had his beard professionally trimmed, along with his hair, and she decided that he looked far more like a successful businessman than a conservative corporate lawyer.

Deirdre, who'd had a walking cast put on to replace the original, wore a long white dress, the simplicity of which was a perfect foil for her natural good looks. She'd applied a minimum of makeup—touches each of blusher, mascara, eyeliner and shadow—and though never one to lean heavily toward jewelry, she'd taken pride in wearing the pearl earrings and matching necklace that her father had given her for her twenty-first birthday.

The ceremony was short and sweet, and Deirdre was all smiles as she circulated through the luncheon reception on the arm of her new husband. He'd given her a stunning gold wedding band, as simple as her gown, with a tracing of diamond chips forming a central circle, but she would have been happy with something from the five-and-dime, as long as it told her they were married. Though he still hadn't said the words, she was sure she'd seen love in his eyes throughout that day, and it was the proverbial frosting on the cake.

THE NEXT FEW WEEKS were hectic ones. Neil threw himself fully into Joyce Enterprises, determined to familiarize himself with every aspect of the business. Sandra readily accepted him; not only was she relieved to have the brunt of the load taken from her shoulders, but Deirdre suspected that she was enthralled by Neil. And rightly so. He exuded confidence and was charming not only to Sandra, but to the uncles, as well. If he came home exhausted at night, Deirdre was more than willing to understand. She was also more than willing to make a challenge out of reviving him, which she did with notable success.

He kept her abreast with what was happening at work, sharing his observations, discussing his plans. And he was even eager to hear about the progress at the house, the redecorating of which she was orchestrating with an enthusiasm that surprised her. She'd never seen herself as a decorator. When she'd moved into her town house she'd simply papered and carpeted to suit herself. Knowing that Neil approved of her taste was a major stimulant—that and knowing the house she now decorated was for the two of them.

By the time they moved in three weeks after the wedding, Deirdre was reeling with confidence. A week later her cast came off, and if that confidence faltered when she experienced a fair amount of pain, Neil was the one to offer encouragement. He personally helped her with the exercises the doctor had outlined, and when those exercise sessions ended more often than not in lovemaking, Deirdre wasn't about to complain. In lieu of verbally professing their love for each other, this physical bonding was crucial to her.

Deirdre put off returning to work, knowing that her leg wasn't ready. Strangely, she didn't miss it as much as she'd thought she would, but, then, between setting up the house and joining Neil for those social engagements he'd warned her would be inevitable, she had little time to miss much of anything.

Strangely, she didn't mind the social engagements, either. But, then, she was with Neil. He never failed to compliment her on the way she looked; as a result, she found that dressing up wasn't as odious as it had been in the past. Moreover, he was the perfect host, drawing her into conversations with their guests such that she experienced far less pain on that score than she'd anticipated.

Neil was exceedingly satisfied with the way things had worked out. Deirdre was as wonderful a wife as she'd been a lover, and as they'd left most of the bickering behind in Maine, he found her to be a thoroughly amiable companion. The only thing that bothered him from time to time was his awareness of the agreement they'd struck. He wanted to think that they were together out of love, not simply taking advantage of a mutually beneficial arrangement. Since the latter was what had brought about this marriage, he went through passing periods of doubt regarding Deirdre's feelings for him.

He had no such self-doubt when it came to Joyce Enterprises. The work was interesting and challenging, and he seemed to have a natural affinity for it. As he'd intended, he brought in a highly experienced executive from a Midwest corporation. Together they mapped out a strategy for keeping Joyce Enterprises not only running smoothly but growing, as well. Between them, they provided the vision that had been lacking since Deirdre's father's death.

Deirdre was thrilled. Her faith in Neil had been justified.

Maria Joyce was likewise pleased, though she made sure Deirdre knew of the risks involved. "I checked up on Neil," she informed her daughter when the two were having lunch at a downtown restaurant one day. "Neither of you was fully honest with me about his past."

Deirdre, who'd been savoring her victory, paused. "We were honest."

"You didn't tell me about Wittnauer-Douglass."

"There wasn't anything to tell. He had a bad experience with one client and was forced to terminate that particular relationship, but it was an isolated incident. He did the same kind of quality work for Wittnauer-Douglass that he did for the rest of his clients."

"According to my friend Bess Hamilton, whose husband is on the board at Wittnauer-Douglass, Neil took part in some unethical dealings."

Deirdre's anger was quick to rise. "If Bess Hamilton's husband was on the board, *he* was involved in the unethical dealings. Neil resigned because he wouldn't have anything to do with it!"

"That wasn't what Bess said."

"And who do you choose to believe, your friend or your son-in-law?"

Maria's gaze didn't waver. "I don't have much choice, do I? Neil is firmly entrenched in the running of our business—"

"And he's doing an excellent job. You can't deny it."

"But I have to wonder what his motives are. From what Bess said, he was washed out in Hartford."

"He wasn't *washed out*. His two associates are doing fantastically well with the business he left them, and if it hadn't been for his own urgings, those clients would have left in a minute and gone elsewhere. They had faith in Neil, which is why they followed his recommendation and stayed with the firm."

Maria wasn't about to be fully convinced. "Still, he got a good thing going for him when he married you. It was a shrewd move."

"What are you trying to say, Mother?" Deirdre asked through gritted teeth.

"Just that I think you ought to be careful. I think we all ought to be careful. He may be trying to take over Joyce Enterprises and sweep it away from us."

"Neil wouldn't do that."

"How do you know?"

"Because I'm *married* to him. Because I *know* him."

"You love him, and love sometimes clouds people's judgment."

"Not in this case. I trust him." She also knew of the papers she'd signed before she and Neil had been married, but she didn't feel that was any of her mother's business. "And I'd think that if you can't find it in yourself to trust him, as well, the least you can do is appreciate him. He's taken a load off all our backs, and what he's doing with Joyce Enterprises would have made Dad proud."

Maria had nothing to say on that score, so she changed the subject. Her words, however, lingered for a long time in Deirdre's mind.

Deirdre had meant what she'd said—that she trusted Neil. There were times, though, when she wondered about the energy he was pouring into the business. Rarely did a night pass when he didn't bring a project of some form home from the office with him. The enthusiasm he had for his work seemed boundless....

Perhaps, Deirdre mused, she was simply jealous. She recalled the days they'd spent in Maine, and there were times when she wished for them again. Neil had been totally devoted to her there; here she had to share him with a very demanding job. She recalled his saying that he'd never married before because the law was such a demanding mistress. At the time she'd argued that the right woman had simply never come along.

Now she wondered if *she* was the right woman, and let her insecurities suggest that she might not be. Yes, Neil was warm and affectionate. Yes, he put aside his work when she came to talk with him. Yes, he was patient with her frustration when her leg seemed to take inordinately long in healing.

But he went off to work quite happily each morning. And he never said that he loved her.

Then again, she realized, maybe her unease was reflective of nothing more than the changes her life had undergone in a few short months. The work on the house was now finished. It was furnished to their mutual satisfaction in the style of understated sophistication that Deirdre had never before thought of as a style; it was merely the way she wanted to live. She wasn't one to spend hours simply looking at the finished product or wandering from one room to another, and the demands Neil made on her for evening engagements weren't enough to occupy her time.

As time passed she grew restless.

She started going to the health club. Though she probably could have taught, she didn't want to. She felt tired. Her leg, though better, still bothered her. She began to wonder whether her compulsion to teach had been directly tied to her need to escape Joyce Enterprises. Since that need was no longer there the compulsion had faded.

She sat at home for long hours, missing Neil, wondering what to do with herself. She lunched with friends, but that brought no lasting relief from her malaise. She took part in the planning of a ten-kilometer charity run, but that occupied far too little of her time.

Finally, on impulse one day, she flew down to meet Victoria for lunch. They hadn't seen each other since the wedding, which Victoria had proudly and delightedly attended, and Deirdre was counting on her friend to bolster her morale.

"How long have you know Neil?" Deirdre asked, broaching the topic as soon as the waiter had left with their order.

"Three years," Victoria answered, cocking her head to the side. "Why do you ask?"

"Did you know him well during that time?"

"We didn't see each other often, but if I were to judge from the quality of the time we spent together, I'd say we were close." She pursed her lips. "Something's up, Dee. Spill it."

Deirdre shrugged, absently playing with the moisture on the outside of her water glass. "I don't know. It's just that everything between us happened so fast. I sometimes wonder if we rushed things."

"You have doubts about Neil?"

"No. Well, maybe once in a while. My mother said something a few weeks ago that bothered me, something about Neil—"

"Your mother," Victoria scoffed. "Your mother is a good friend of mine, but that doesn't mean I can't see her faults. She's one of those people who are never satisfied. You take her too seriously, Dee. I've told you that before."

"I know. But I can't help hearing her little 'words of wisdom.'"

"You may have to hear them. You don't have to heed them."

"But it's like they niggle in the back of my mind and they refuse to go away." She raised beseeching eyes to her friend. "Victoria, do you think Neil is ambitious?"

"I should hope so. No one is successful if he isn't ambitious."

"Ruthlessly so? Would you call Neil ruthlessly ambitious?"

Victoria didn't have to think about that. "No. Unequivocally. Neil is not a ruthless person. If anything, the opposite is true. If he had a little more of the bastard in him, he might not have had that problem with Wittnauer-Douglass."

"If he hadn't had that," Deirdre pointed out with a lopsided grin, "he'd never have run off to Maine and I'd never have met him, so I can't be sorry about Wittnauer-Douglass." Her grin faded. "It's just that my mother learned about all that, and she suggested that Neil might be out for himself when it comes to Joyce Enterprises."

"Is that what you think?"

"No. At least, I want to think that it isn't so. But he's taken to his work with such . . . such *glee*, and there are times when I wish he showered more of that glee on me."

"You can't have it both ways, Dee. If he's to turn Joyce Enterprises around, he's going to have to put in the hours. Take my word for it, though. Neil Hersey has nothing but the most upstanding intentions when it comes to your business. I don't think there's a selfish bone in that man's body. Did he ever tell you what he did for my niece?"

Deirdre frowned. "No. He never mentioned your niece."

"He wouldn't. That's his way."

"Well? What did he do?"

"A while ago, my niece got involved in a criminal matter. The girl was only nineteen at the time, and her mother—my sister—was frantic. They live in a small town in western Connecticut and aren't very well off, and they didn't know where to turn for help. I called Neil, knowing that criminal law wasn't his specialty but hoping that he'd be able to refer us to a capable person. Not only did he do that, but he personally involved himself in the case, and then, when the other lawyer would have given him a referral fee, he insisted that the man deduct it from the fee he charged my sister—a fee, mind you, that was on the low side, anyway, considering that my niece got away with nothing but probation. Now—" she tipped up her chin "—if Neil were only out for himself, would he have done all that for my niece?"

Deirdre felt a rush of pride in her husband. "No. And I know that he's always done charity work. It's just that the situation with us is so different. There's so much at stake for him now."

"I doubt he'd consider anything more important than your love."

Deirdre held her breath.

"Dee? You do love him, don't you?"

"Oh, yes!"

"But . . . ?"

"I'm not sure he loves me."

"Are you kidding?"

Deirdre responded defensively. "No, I'm not kidding. He's never told me he loved me. Our marriage was . . . was . . . expedient, and that was his own word."

Victoria pressed a calming hand on her arm. "Look, sweetheart, I know enough about each of your situations to realize that your getting married solved certain problems for you both. But I saw Neil at your wedding, and if that man wasn't in love, I'll turn in my matchmaker badge." She paused. "What does he say when you tell him that you love him?"

Deirdre didn't have to answer. Guilt was written all over her face.

"My Lord, Dee. Why not? You're no wilting pansy!"

"But I don't want to pressure him. Worse, I don't want to say it and not have him say it back. And anyway, when he's home there's so much else we talk about, and then we don't want to talk at all. . . ."

Victoria shot her a knowing grin. "That's more like it." She raised her eyes when the waiter approached with their plates, and waited until he'd deposited the meal and gone. "So, Neil is very busy with work, and you're feeling lonesome."

"Yes."

"Have you told him that?"

"No."

Victoria cast pleading eyes toward the ornate ceiling high overhead. "I know I shouldn't ask this, but why not?"

"Because in the first place, I don't want to sound like a complainer. When we first got to Maine, that was all

I did—bitch at him, and everything else in sight. Then our relationship gelled, and I stopped griping. I liked myself a lot more then. I don't want to go back to that other way." She paused for an exaggerated breath. "And in the second place, there's nothing he can do about it."

"He can reassure you, maybe help find something to keep you busy."

Deirdre shook her head sadly. "I don't know, Victoria. I look at you and I'm envious. When you finish one thing you start another. I used to have a million and one things to do with my day, but now I can't seem to find anything that tempts me."

"You want to be with Neil. Everything else is...blah. So why don't you work part-time at the office?"

"That'd be tantamount to surrender. I swore I'd never work there."

"And you're so rigid that you can't reconsider, particularly knowing that working there now would be out of choice, rather than need?"

Deirdre didn't respond immediately; she sat absently nudging her cold salmon with a fork. "Put that way, I sound pretty childish."

"If the shoe fits . . ."

"I don't know, Victoria. I'm not sure that's what I want, either."

"Do me a favor, Dee, and talk with Neil? He's a patient man. Really, he is. And he's resourceful. Most important, he's your husband. He wants you to be happy." She speared a firm green bean and held it over her plate. "Will you?"

"I'll try."

"Don't try. *Do* it!"

DEIRDRE WOULD HAVE done it that night, had Neil not offered her a solution before she'd been able to utter a word. He'd come home particularly tired, and they were relaxing in the living room, sharing a glass of wine.

"I need your help, Deirdre," he announced in a businesslike tone.

"There's a problem at the office?"

He nodded. "In personnel. Art Brickner, our man there, is giving us flack about hiring people to fill in certain gaps. He wanted to bring people up from the ranks, and I agree with him in theory, except that in several of these cases there simply is no one to bring up from the ranks. Most of his resistance is to new blood, and I fall prominently in that category. Art was one of your father's original men."

"I know . . . But how can I help?"

"Work with him. Ease him through the transition. He's a good man—"

"He's stodgy."

Neil chuckled. "Yes, he's stodgy, but his instincts are good, and your presence in his office might just remind him that, contrary to what he fears, all is not going down the tubes at Joyce Enterprises."

"Oh, Neil . . . what do I know about personnel?"

"You have common sense, and a feel for the company. Art will take care of the mechanics, while you handle the, uh, the spiritual end. What do you think?"

"I think," she said, studying the features she adored so much, "that you look exhausted. You're working too hard, Neil."

Loosening his necktie, he sank deeper into the sofa. "You're right. But it has to be done." His eyes narrowed. "You look exhausted, too. Was it running down to New York to have lunch with Victoria?"

"Uh-uh. I'm tired from having too much time on my hands."

"Then helping Art could be just the thing."

"Neil—"

"You wouldn't have to work full-time, only twenty hours a week or so."

"But I—"

"You could wear whatever you wanted, since you wouldn't be in the limelight."

"But what—"

"I'd even pay you." He grinned broadly. "How does that sound?"

She sighed, stared at him in exasperation for a minute, then took his silent offer and settled under the arm he held out. "When you smile at me like that, Neil Hersey, I'm a goner. But you know that, don't you, which is why you do it! I'm a sucker. That's all. A real sucker."

"Then you will work?"

"Yes, I will work."

"And you'll tell me if it turns out to be too much?"

"It won't turn out to be too much. I'm young. I'm full of energy. I'm brimming with enthusiasm...."

BUT IT DID TURN OUT to be too much—or rather, it put a strain on Deirdre that she hadn't expected. She worked from nine to two every day, and was positively drained. After a week of mornings when she couldn't seem to get going, she began coming in at ten. Even then she was dragging by the time Neil arrived home at night.

Witnessing her struggle, Neil grew more and more tense. He waited for her to come to him, to broach the subject, but she didn't. Finally, after two weeks of helplessness, he took matters into his own hands.

Arriving home early from work, he found Deirdre curled beneath an afghan on their king-size bed, sound asleep. He sat on the bed beside her, leaned down and kissed her cheek.

Her lashes fluttered, then rose. "Neil!" she whispered, pushing herself up. "I'm sorry. I never dreamed you'd be home this early!"

He pulled a bouquet of flowers—actually, three roses and an assortment of greens—from behind him. "For you."

Groggy still, she looked from him to the roses and back, smiling at last. "They're lovely. Any special occasion?"

"Mmm-hmm. Today's the day we admit that you're pregnant."

Deirdre's smile vanished, as did what little color had been on her cheeks. She lay back on the bed, closed her eyes and spoke in a very small voice. "How did you guess?"

Neil was stricken by the unhappiness he saw on Deirdre's face. He'd assumed that she'd been afraid to tell him—though he didn't know why—but apparently there was more than fear involved. He answered her quietly. "We've been married for nearly three months, and during that time you haven't had a single period."

"I'm an athlete," she pointed out. "That can do strange things to a woman's system."

"You're constantly tired. Even the slightest activity exhausts you."

"It's everything that's happened in the past few months. I'm on emotional overload."

"And the greater fullness of your breasts?" he asked, his voice deep and low. "And the slight thickening of your waist? Things that nobody else sees, I do. Come on, Deirdre. Let's face the facts. You're pregnant. Is it so awful?"

She focused tired eyes on him. "I feel so lousy right now that, yes, it's awful."

"Then you agree that it's true?"

"It's true."

"But you haven't been to a doctor."

"No."

"Why, Deirdre? Don't you want to have a baby?"

"I do!" she cried, then lowered her voice. "It's just that, on top of everything else, it's so sudden...."

"We weren't using any birth control. You had to know there was a possibility this would happen."

"How did you know I wasn't using birth control?" she countered, being contrary.

"Deirdre, I was with you constantly. I would have known."

"Not if I'd had an IUD."

"But you didn't have one, and you're pregnant now!"

"Thanks to you. If you knew I wasn't using anything, why didn't *you* use something?"

"Deirdre, I do not pack prophylactics as a matter of habit. The last thing I expected when I went up to Maine was that I'd be with a woman."

"So neither of us was prepared, and both of us knew it, and we did nothing, and look what happened."

"I don't think it's such a horrible situation, Deirdre."

"You don't?"

"Of course not."

"You don't feel that it's just another burden on your shoulders?"

"Have I ever talked of burdens?"

"No. But they're there."

"This one's a nice one. I told you I wanted children."

"'Someday,' you said."

"Then 'someday' is now. And the more I think about it, the happier I am." Scooping her up, he tucked her against him. "I know you're not feeling great, Deirdre, but once you see a doctor and he gives you vitamins, and once you pass the initial few months, you'll feel better."

To Deirdre's dismay, she began to cry. Her fingers closed around the lapel of his suit jacket, and she buried her face in his shirt.

"I'll be . . . be fat."

"You'll be beautiful."

"You'll . . . you'll be stuck with me."

"I'm not complaining."

"You're being so . . . kind."

"You're being such a ninny." He hugged her, trying his best to absorb whatever pain she was feeling. He knew she'd been through a lot, and that having a baby at a later time would probably have been better for her, but he wasn't sorry. It bound her all the closer to him.

Weeping softly, Deirdre was thinking similar thoughts. Oh, yes, she wanted the baby, but because it was Neil's, more than for any other reason. When she thought of it, having his baby made the tie between them even more permanent than marriage. It was both a reassuring and a frightening thought, because if something went wrong and Neil decided he'd had enough, a wholly innocent child would be affected.

The scent of roses by her nose interrupted her sniffles. She opened her eyes and saw Neil touch each bloom.

"One for you, one for me, one for baby. A nice bunch, don't you think?"

His sweetness brought a helpless smile to Deirdre's wet face. "A very nice bunch."

Later, she told herself, she'd watch for the thorns. For now, she was too tired to do anything but relax in Neil's arms.

9

ONCE DEIRDRE accepted the fact of her pregnancy, she was better able to cope. She saw a doctor and began a regimen of vitamins that compensated for what the baby demanded of her body. She continued working with Art Brickner, adjusting her hours to accommodate her need for sleep.

Neil seemed legitimately pleased about the baby, and that relieved her most of all. In turn, she made up her mind to do everything in her power to make their marriage work.

When she was at the office, she dressed accordingly, intent on making Neil proud. When she was at home she planned their meals and coordinated the various cleaning efforts so that the house was always immaculate should Neil decide to bring people home at the last minute. At Neil's insistence, though, they'd hired a maid to help. She resumed her visits to the health club—the doctor had okayed that—and though she didn't teach, she took part in classes. She swam. She diligently kept herself in shape—as much as a woman with a slowly growing belly could.

And she never argued with Neil. She didn't complain when he was delayed for several hours at the office and dinner was held up. She didn't say a word when he had to go away on a business trip. She didn't nag him to take time off from work to play tennis with her. She graciously attended cocktail parties and dinners, and when she and Neil were finally alone at night, she did her very best to satisfy him, both physically and emotionally.

But because she refused to give him any cause for displeasure, the frustration that had built within her had nowhere to go. She wished he didn't work so hard, but she didn't say so. She yearned for time alone with him—even their weekends revolved around business demands—but she didn't say so. She ached, positively ached to hear him say that he loved her, but she didn't say so, and he didn't tell her what she wanted to hear. She felt as if she were walking a tightrope.

The tightrope began to fray when her mother dropped in one morning. Deirdre was getting ready to leave for work.

"Have you heard his latest scheme?" Maria asked with an arrogance Deirdre found all too familiar. They were standing in the front hall; Deirdre knew enough not to invite her mother to sit, or she'd be in for an even longer siege.

"That depends on which scheme it is," Deirdre countered with confidence. "Neil's had a lot of them lately, and they're all very promising."

"This one isn't."

"Which one?"

"He's bidding on a government contract for the electronics division."

Deirdre had known that. "Is there a problem?" she asked blandly.

"We've never bid for government contracts. We've always devoted ourselves to the private sector."

"That doesn't mean we can't change now, if doing so will be good for the company."

"But will it? That's the question. Is Neil bidding for that contract because it will be good for the company or for him?"

"Aren't they one and the same?" Deirdre asked, ignoring her mother's barely veiled reference to the earlier accusation she'd made.

"Not by a long shot. You may not know it, but one of the other bidders is Wittnauer-Douglass."

Deirdre hadn't known it. She ignored the frisson of anxiety that shivered through her. "I'm sure there are many other bidders—"

"None Neil holds a grudge against."

"Neil doesn't hold a grudge against Wittnauer-Douglass," Deirdre insisted. "What happened there is done. He is very successful in what he's doing now. I think you're way off base."

"You've thought that from the start, when I told you to be careful, but this is the evidence I need."

"Evidence? What evidence?"

"Your husband is involving Joyce Enterprises in something solely for the sake of avenging himself. He would never be bidding for a government contract if it weren't for that. Think about it. Isn't it awfully suspicious that the first time we do anything of this sort, a major competitor is the very one Neil has a gripe against?"

Deirdre set her purse down on the table. "Do you know the details, Mother? Who submitted a bid first, Wittnauer-Douglass or Joyce Enterprises?"

Maria fumbled with the collar of her sable coat. "I don't know that. How could I possibly know that!"

"If it's evidence you're looking for, that'd be a place to start. If Neil submitted his bid first, without ever knowing that Wittnauer-Douglass would be a competitor, his innocence would be obvious."

"The rest of the evidence is against him."

Deirdre was losing her patience. "What evidence?"

"Deirdre," her mother said, sighing. "Think. Neil met you at a time when he needed a change of location and occupation."

"He did not need—"

"He latched onto what you had to offer, married you as quickly as possible and set about implementing his plans."

"The plans he implemented were for the resurgence of Joyce Enterprises, and he's done a remarkable job! He's done us a favor!"

"He's done himself a favor. Look at it objectively. He's at the helm of a successful corporation. He's become so well respected in the community that the two of you are in demand at all the parties that matter—"

"If you had any sense of appreciation, Mother, you'd spend your time tallying all he's done for *you*. He's married the more undesirable of your two daughters and is about to give you a grandchild. He's taken responsibility for the family business—and even gotten *me* involved in it. What more do you want?"

"I want Joyce Enterprises to remain in the black."

"And you think that bidding on a government contract will prevent that?" Deirdre asked in disbelief. "He's just bidding."

"If he wants that contract badly enough, he'll bid low enough to undercut Wittnauer-Douglass, and if he does that, he could jeopardize our financial status."

"And if he does that," Deirdre pointed out angrily, "he'll be jeopardizing the very position he's built for himself. It doesn't make sense, Mother. You're being illogical."

"It's a risk—his bidding for that contract."

"There's always a risk if the prize is worth anything. If Neil only stuck with what was safe, the business would be at a standstill."

"He's being rash. I think you should talk with him."

Deirdre had had enough. "I don't have to listen to this." She snatched up her purse, took her coat from the nearby chair and headed for the door. "You can stay if you like. I have to get to work."

Deirdre might have been fine had the conversation she'd had with her mother been the only one of its kind. But several days later, Art Brickner raised the issue, complaining that Neil had spoken with him about hiring an enlarged cadre of workers if the government contract came through. Art questioned both the logistics and the wisdom of what Neil proposed, and all Deirdre could do was to support Neil and insist that his plan was sound.

Several days after that, she was approached by one of the long-standing vice presidents of the company, who, too, had doubts as to the direction in which Joyce was headed. Again Deirdre expressed her support for

Neil, sensing that what she was hearing was simply a resistance to change, but she grew increasingly uncomfortable.

She didn't tell Neil about any of the three discussions. She didn't want to anger him by suggesting that she had doubts, when, in fact, she had no qualms about the viability of winning and working through a government contract. What bothered her was the possibility that his motives weren't entirely pure, that, as her mother had suggested, he was being driven by a desire for revenge. She tried to ignore such thoughts, but they wouldn't leave her.

At the root of the matter were the doubts she had regarding their relationship. Oh, they were close. They said all the right things, did all the right things. To the outside world—and to themselves, on one level—they were a loving couple. If she recalled the original reasons for their marriage, though, as she did with increasing frequency, she couldn't help but question what it was that drove Neil. His questionable motives bothered her far more than the prospect of any contract, government or otherwise.

So she walked the tightrope. On one end was what she wanted; on the other what she thought Neil wanted. The rope frayed. It finally snapped when he arrived home unexpectedly one afternoon. She was instantly pleased, delighted by the thought of spending stolen time with him. The sight of him—ruggedly handsome, with his beard offsetting his more formal suit—never failed to excite her, as did the inevitable kiss with which he greeted her.

Threading his arm through hers, he led her into the den. When he held her back, though, the look of tension on his face told her something was amiss.

"I need a favor, Deirdre. I have to run to Washington for a meeting tonight. Do you think you could handle the dinner party on your own?"

They'd long ago invited three couples to join them at a restaurant in town. Deirdre knew the couples. They weren't her favorite people.

Her face fell. "Oh, Neil . . . do you have to go?"

"I do. It's important." He felt like a heel, but there was no way around it.

"But so sudden. You were planning to go down for the presentation tomorrow morning, anyway. Can't you have this meeting then?"

"Not if I want the presentation to be the best it can be."

"It will be. You've been working on it for weeks."

"I want that contract," he stated, then coaxed her more gently. "Come on. You can handle things at the restaurant."

"You know how I hate dinners like that."

"I know that you manage them beautifully." She'd proved it in the past weeks, and he'd been proud of her.

"With you by my side. But you won't be, which makes the whole thing that much more distasteful."

"I'm asking for your help. I can't be two places at once."

Annoyances, past and present, rose within her. She left his side, grabbed a throw pillow from the sofa and began to fluff it with a vengeance. "And you choose to be in Washington. If you wanted to be here, you could

send someone else to Washington. Why can't Ben go?"
Ben Tillotson was the executive Neil had brought in
from the midwest.

"Ben's daughter is visiting from Seattle. He feels
badly enough that he has to leave her tomorrow."

"Well, what about me? You have to leave me tomorrow, too." She dropped the first pillow and started on
another.

"It's my responsibility before it's Ben's."

"Then if Ben can't make it, why don't you let Thor
go?" Thor VanNess headed the electronics division. In
Deirdre's mind, he'd be the perfect one to attend the
meeting.

"Thor is fantastic at what he does, but he is not a
diplomat, and the meeting tonight is going to involve
a fair share of diplomacy."

"And you're the only diplomat at Joyce?"

Her sarcasm was a sharp prod, poking holes in Neil's
patience. "Deirdre," he said, sighing, "you're making
too much out of a single meeting. If you want, I can
have my secretary call and cancel the dinner party, but
I'd hoped that wouldn't be necessary. Believe me, I've
looked for other outs. I've tried to think of someone else
who can get the job done tonight in Washington, but
there is no one else. It's *my responsibility*."

She tossed the second pillow on the sofa and leaned
forward to straighten a small watercolor that hung on
the wall. "Then you take too much on your own shoulders. I was under the assumption that delegation was
critical to the smooth functioning of a corporation this
size." She lowered her voice in an attempt to curb her
temper. Yes, she was making too much out of a single

meeting, but it had become a matter of principle. She faced him head-on. "Send someone else. Anyone else."

"I can't, Deirdre. It's as simple as that."

"No, it's not," she declared, unable to hold it in any longer. "It's not simple at all. You put your work before every other thing in our lives, which shows where *your* priorities lie."

Neil bowed his head and rubbed the back of his neck. "You're being unfair," he said quietly.

"Unfair? Or selfish? Well, maybe it's about time!" She stalked to the large ship's clock that hung on another wall, took a tool from its side, opened it and angrily began to wind it.

"Take it easy, babe. You're making a mountain out of—"

"I am not!"

"You're getting upset." His gaze fell to the tiny swell just visible in profile beneath her oversized sweater. "It's not good for you *or* the baby."

She turned to glare at him. "That's where you're wrong. It's the *best* thing for me, and therefore for the baby, because I can't pretend anymore. I'm being torn apart inside."

Neil stiffened. "What are you talking about?"

"I can't stand this, Neil. I've tried to be the perfect wife for you. I've done all the things I swore I'd never do, and I've done them without argument because I wanted to please you. I wanted to make this marriage work."

"I thought it was working. Do you mean to tell me you were faking it all?"

She scrunched up her face in frustration. "I wasn't faking it. On one level the marriage does work. But there has to be more. There has to be total communication. You discuss the business with me, but I don't know what you're really thinking or feeling. There are times when I feel totally left out of what's happening."

"You could ask more."

"You could offer more."

"Damn it, Deirdre, how do I know what you want if you don't ask?"

"Don't you know me well enough to know what I want without my having to ask?"

"No!" he exploded, angry now himself. "I thought you wanted me to make a go of your damned business, but it looks like I was wrong. I've been busting my ass in the office racking my brain, dipping into resources I didn't know I had, looking for one way, then another to make Joyce Enterprises stronger."

For an instant she was taken back. "I thought you enjoyed the work."

"I do enjoy the work, but that's because I've been successful. I've felt good knowing that I was carrying out my part of the bargain, knowing that I had the business moving again. Every bit of my satisfaction relates directly or indirectly to you."

Deirdre eyed him skeptically. "Are you sure? Isn't there a little satisfaction that relates solely to you?"

"I suppose," he answered, rubbing his bearded cheek. "If I stand back and look at what I've been able to do in a few short months, yes, I'm proud of myself. I'm a lawyer by training, not a businessman, yet I've taken on entrepreneurial tasks that two, four, six years ago I'd never have dared tackle."

"But you have now. Why?"

Neil was still for a moment, his tone almost puzzled when he spoke. "It was part of the agreement we made."

"No. Go back further." Her hand tightened around the clock tool. "Why did we make that agreement?"

"Because you needed me and I needed you."

"That's right. And I guess it's one of the things that's been eating at me. You needed a means of reestablishing yourself after what happened in Hartford. You came in here, took over the reins, and you've done more with this company than anyone else—including my father—has done in years. You've done everything I expected, and more. Why, Neil? Why so much?"

"That's an absurd question," he snapped. "If there are things to be done, I believe in doing them. Yes, I could have stopped thinking a while ago, and Joyce Enterprises still would have been in far better shape than it had been. But I've seen potential in the company. I'm trying to realize it."

Replacing the clock tool, Deirdre moved to a plant hanging by the window and began to pick dried leaves from it. "Or are you trying to prove to Wittnauer-Douglass that you can beat them at their own game?"

"What?" He tipped his head and narrowed one eye. "What are you talking about?"

"This government contract. You've told me all about your end of it, and I've been in favor of it. What you didn't tell me was that Wittnauer-Douglass is bidding for the same contract." She crushed the dried leaves in her hand. "My *mother* had to tell me that, and at the same time she leveled a pretty harsh accusation."

"Your mother's leveled accusations before, and they've proved unfounded." He was staring hard at Deirdre. When she reached toward the plant again, he bellowed, "Leave the damn plant alone, Deirdre. I want your full attention right now."

Slowly she turned to face him, but she didn't say a word, because his expression was suddenly one of fury, reminiscent of their first days in Maine, but worse.

His lips were thinned; tension radiated from the bridge of his nose. "You think that I'm going for this contract to get even with Wittnauer-Douglass!" he spat, his eyes widening. "You actually think that I'm out for revenge, that everything I've done since we've been married has been with this in mind! I don't believe you, Deirdre! Where have you *been* all these weeks?"

She grew defensive. "I didn't say I thought that. I said my mother thought that."

"But you're raising it with me now, which means that you have your own doubts."

"Yes, I have my doubts! I've stood behind you one hundred percent, defending you before my mother, before Art Brickner, before others of my father's people who've approached me with questions. I've been as strong an advocate as I can possibly be, but after a while all I can think of is that our marriage was *expedient*." She covered her face with one rigid hand and spoke into her palm. "I hate that word. God, do I hate that word."

"Then why do you use it?" he yelled back.

She dropped her hand. "Because *you* used it, and it's stuck in my mind like glue, and I try to shake it off, but it won't let go! We married for the wrong reasons, Neil, and it's about time we faced it. I can't go on this way. It's driving me nuts!"

Neil thrust a hand through his hair. "Driving *you* nuts! Do you think it's any different for me? I've tried my best to make things work, and I thought they were working. Now I find out that every one of my efforts has been in vain. I thought you trusted me, but maybe all you wanted was someone to bail you out. Now that I've done that, I'm expendable. Is that it?"

"No! I never said that!"

"Then what are you saying? What in the hell do you want?"

She was shaking—in anger, in frustration, in heartache. Clenching her fists by her sides, she cried, "I want it *all*! I don't want an expedient marriage! I never did! I want *love*, Neil! Damn it, *I want the real thing*!"

Neil was far from steady himself. Equal parts of tension, fear and anguish thrummed through his body, clouding his mind, robbing him of the thoughts, much less the words to fight her. Feeling more impotent than he'd ever felt in his life, he turned and stormed from the room.

Deirdre wrapped her arms around her middle and tried to control the wild hammering of her heart. She heard the front door slam, then, moments later, the angry rev of the LeBaron. It had long since faded into silence before she began to move in small, dazed steps, working her way slowly toward her favorite room, the loft above the garage.

Late-afternoon sun filtered in across the polished wood floor, splashing on bare stucco walls with a cheeriness that eluded her at the moment. Her cassette player and a pile of tapes lay in one corner. She'd often used the room for exercise, though what she'd really hoped was that one day it would be a playroom for their children.

Now all that seemed in doubt.

Carefully easing herself down onto the cushioned sill of the arched window, she tucked her knees up, pressed her forehead to them and began to cry.

Neil didn't love her. If he had, he'd have said so. She'd given him the opening; she'd told him what she wanted. And he'd left her. He didn't love her.

And their future? A big, fat question mark. In some respects they were back where they'd started when they'd first arrived on Victoria's island.

What had she wanted, really wanted then? Love. She hadn't realized it at the time, but in the weeks since, she realized that everything else would have fallen into place if she'd found love. She could teach, or not. She could work at Joyce Enterprises, or not. The one thing that held meaning was love.

NEIL DROVE AROUND for hours. He stopped at a pay phone to call the office, but he had no desire to show up there. He had no desire to go to Washington. He had no desire to bid for, much less win, that government contract he'd sought. He had no desire to do anything . . . but return to Deirdre.

That was the one thing that became eminently clear with the miles he put on his odometer. Deirdre was all that mattered in his life.

He relived their meeting in Maine, their arguments, their eventual coming to terms with each other. He reviewed the months they'd been married and all that had happened, both personally and professionally, during that time. But mostly he replayed the scene he'd had with Deirdre that day. He heard her words, pondered them, analyzed them.

And it occurred to him that he was possibly on the verge of making the biggest mistake of his life.

Stopping the car in the middle of the street, he ignored the honking of horns, made a U-turn and mentally mapped the fastest route back to the house. When he arrived, it was nearly ten o'clock. The house was every bit as dark as the night was, and for a minute he feared he was too late. Then his headlights illumined Deirdre's car, parked as unobtrusively as she'd left it beneath the huge maple tree. Pulling up behind it, he jumped from his own and ran inside.

"Deirdre?" he called, flipping lights on in each of the ground floor rooms. "Deirdre!" There was no anger in his voice, simply worry. With the irrational fear of a man in love, he conjured up every one of the dreadful things that might have happened to her during his absence. She was upset. She was pregnant. Oh, God...

Taking the stairs two at a time, he searched their bedroom, then the others. Only when there was still no sign of her did he stop to think. Then, praying that he'd find her there, he headed for the loft.

"Deirdre?" Fearfully he said her name as he switched on the light, then caught his breath when he saw her curled on the window seat, her head having fallen against the windowpane. In the seconds it took him to cross to her, he added even more dreadful things to his list of fears.

Lowering himself by her side, he brushed her cheek with his thumb. Dried tears streaked her skin, but her color was good and she was warm.

"Deirdre?" His voice was soft and shaky. "Wake up, sweetheart. There's something I have to tell you." He smoothed the hair from her forehead, leaned forward to kiss her wheat-hued crown, framed her face with both hands. "Deirdre?"

She took in a hiccuping breath and, frowning, raised heavy lids. Disoriented, she stared at him for a minute, then her eyes opened fully and she pushed herself up against the window frame. "You're back," she whispered.

He smiled gently. "Yes."

"What . . . what happened to Washington?"

"It's not important."

"But the contract—"

"Isn't important."

"But you wanted it—"

"Not as much as I want you." When her eyes filled with confusion and disbelief, he explained. "I've driven around for hours thinking about things, and when I went back over what you said earlier, I realized that I may have got things wrong. I was so convinced that you wanted out of the marriage, that you'd gotten tired of me and it, that I took your words one way, when they could have been taken another." His hands were cupping her head, thumbs stroking the short, smooth strands of hair behind her ears. "I may be wrong again, but I think it's worth the risk."

He took a deep breath. Once there might have been pride involved, but he'd gone well beyond that. Still, he was nervous. His words came out in a rush. "I love you, Deirdre. *That* was why I wanted to marry you in the first place. Anything else that came along with the marriage was nice, but purely secondary. Maybe I've had my guard up, because I never knew for sure why, deep down inside, you agreed to marry me. And I was afraid to ask outright, because I didn't want to know... if you'd married me simply because of our bargain. But what you said earlier set me to thinking. What you said, and the anguish in it, would make sense if you love me and fear that I don't love you back." His eyes grew moist, and his voice shook again. "Do you, Deirdre? Do you love me?"

Tears welled on her lower lids, and her chin quivered. "Very much," she whispered, which was all she could manage because emotion clogged her throat, making further sound impossible.

Neil closed his eyes in relief and hauled her against him. "Oh, Deirdre," he rasped, "we've been so foolish." His arms wound fully around her; hers had found their way beneath his jacket and held him every bit as tightly. "So foolish," he whispered against her hair. "We never said the words. The only words that mattered, and we never said them."

Deirdre's heart was near to bursting. "I love you...love you so much," she whispered brokenly, and raised her eyes to his. "We had so much going for us, and we nearly blew it."

A shudder passed through him. He took her mouth in a fierce kiss, gentling only when he reminded himself that she wasn't going to leave. "When I think of everything else I've had in my life, things I've risked, things I've lost, they seem so unimportant now. You're what matters. This is where you belong, in my arms. And I belong in yours."

"I know," she said, and buried her face against his neck. The scent of him was familiar and dear; it was an aphrodisiac in times of passion, a soothing balm in times of emotional need. She breathed deeply of it, and her face blossomed into a smile. Then the smile faded, replaced by a look of horror. "Neil!" She pushed back from his arms. "The dinner party! They'll have gone to the restaurant and we've stood them up!"

He chuckled. "Not to worry. I called my secretary and had her cancel on our behalf. We'll make it another time. Together."

Deirdre wrinkled her nose. "I don't like the Emerys. He is an arrogant bore, and she has bad breath." Neil laughed aloud, but she hadn't finished. "And Donald Lutz is always checking out the room, on the lookout for someone important to greet, while that wife of his can't take her hand off the chunky emerald ring she wears. And as for the Spellmans, they're—"

Neil put a hand over her mouth, but he was grinning. "They're important clients. Once in a while we have to sacrifice our own personal preferences for the sake of the corporation."

"Speaking of which..." She mumbled into his hand, then spoke more clearly, if softly when he removed it. "I don't distrust you, Neil. Everything you've done at Joyce has been good. And I *am* in favor of the government project if it comes through."

"I didn't do it because of Wittnauer-Douglass, Deirdre. I didn't even know they were bidding for the same project."

"That was what I suggested to my mother," Deirdre said, feeling faintly smug. "She's a troublemaker. Do you know that? The woman is a born troublemaker! I never realized it, because I always assumed that she was right and that everything was my fault, but she's been dead wrong about us from the start. Victoria had her pegged. My mother is one of those people who are never satisfied. It may be a little late, but I actually feel sorry for my father. No wonder he poured so much of his time and energy into the business. He was running away from her!"

Hearing her evaluation of her parents' relationship gave Deirdre a moment's pause. Her confidence wavered. "Were you doing that, Neil? Were you running away from me, spending every minute thinking about the business?"

"A good many of those minutes you thought I was thinking about the business, I was thinking about you," he said with a crooked smile. Then the smile vanished. "I wanted to please you. I felt that if I couldn't win your heart, I'd at least win your respect."

"You've had that from the start. And I admire—no, I stand in awe of—what you've done with the business." She sharpened her gaze on him. "But I meant what I said about delegating authority. I want more of your time, Neil! I want to do things with you. I want to go out to romantic little lunches every so often, or play tennis, or take off for the weekend and go...wherever!"

His eyes twinkled. "I think I can manage that."

"And I want to go to Washington with you tomorrow."

"No."

"Why not?"

"Because I'm not going."

She stared at him for a minute. "You're not?"

"No. Ben can handle it."

"But you're the best one for the job! You know it, and I know it."

"But there is a question of conflict of interest."

"I don't believe that! I was angry, or I'd never have even suggested it!"

"Now you're being diplomatic," he teased.

"I am not!"

He grew serious. "I thought a lot about that situation, too, while I was out driving. No, I didn't originally know that we'd be competing against Wittnauer-Douglass for that contract, but I have to admit that when I found out, there was intense satisfaction in it. I mean, we may not get the contract. The bids are sealed, and I have no way of knowing who bid what. The contract may go to Wittnauer-Douglass, or it may go to one of the other bidders. But I did get an inordinate amount of pleasure knowing that Joyce is right up there in the Wittnauer-Douglass league."

"There's nothing wrong with that—"

"But the point is that I have already avenged myself."

"Yes, but through honest hard work and talent. Not just anyone could have done what you've done, Neil. Joyce Enterprises was marking time. You have it moving forward. If you won't take the credit, then I'll take it for you!"

Her pride in him gave him a thrill. "You will, will you?"

"Uh-huh." She thought for a minute. "But what about practicing law. That was what you really wanted to do. Don't you miss it?"

"I've been practicing law at Joyce, but with lots of other things thrown in. I do think it's time Ben and I switch places, though. I want to maintain a position of power, because I've enjoyed having a say in what we do when, but I don't need a fancy title, and I *don't* need the full burden of responsibility I've been carrying." He paused. "But what about you? You haven't been teaching, and that was what you really wanted to do. Don't you miss it?"

"No," she said firmly, then grew pensive. "Maybe I've outgrown it. Maybe the need just isn't there anymore. It filled a void in my life, but the void is gone. Being a helpmate to you is far more satisfying than teaching ever was."

He hugged her. "The things you mentioned before—things we could do together—I want to do them, too, Deirdre. We never did take a honeymoon."

"We had that before we were married."

"But I want another one. A *real* one. You know, a luxurious cottage someplace warm, champagne at sunset, hours lying on the beach in the sun, maid service and laundry service and room service."

Deirdre slanted him a mischievous grin. "What happened to the man who could do it all himself?"

"He wants to be able to concentrate solely on his wife. Is that a crime?"

"You're the lawyer. You tell me."

He never did. Rather, he kissed her with such sweet conviction that she didn't care if they broke every law in the book.

My
Valentine
1994

Celebrate the most romantic day of the year with
MY VALENTINE 1994
a collection of original stories, written by
four of Harlequin's most popular authors...

MARGOT DALTON
MURIEL JENSEN
MARISA CARROLL
KAREN YOUNG

Available in February, wherever
Harlequin Books are sold.

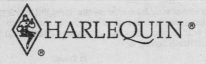

HARLEQUIN®

VAL94

**Fifty red-blooded, white-hot, true-blue hunks
from every State in the Union!**

Look for MEN MADE IN AMERICA! Written by some
of our most poplar authors, these stories feature fifty of
the strongest, sexiest men, each from a different state in
the union!

Two titles available every other month at your favorite
retail outlet.

In January, look for:

DREAM COME TRUE by Ann Major (Florida)
WAY OF THE WILLOW by Linda Shaw (Georgia)

In March, look for:

TANGLED LIES by Anne Stuart (Hawaii)
ROGUE'S VALLEY by Kathleen Creighton (Idaho)

You won't be able to resist MEN MADE IN AMERICA!

Relive the romance...
Harlequin and Silhouette
are proud to present

A program of collections of three complete novels by the most requested
authors with the most requested themes. Be sure to look for one volume each
month with three complete novels by top name authors.

In January:	**WESTERN LOVING**	Susan Fox
		JoAnn Ross
		Barbara Kaye

Loving a cowboy is easy—taming him isn't!

In February:	**LOVER, COME BACK!**	Diana Palmer
		Lisa Jackson
		Patricia Gardner Evans

It was over so long ago—yet now they're calling, "Lover, Come Back!"

In March:	**TEMPERATURE RISING**	JoAnn Ross
		Tess Gerritsen
		Jacqueline Diamond

Falling in love—just what the doctor ordered!

Available at your favorite retail outlet.

REQ-G3

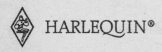

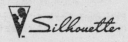

Earth, Wind, Fire, Water
The four elements—but nothing is
more elemental than passion.

PASSION'S QUEST

Join us for *Passion's Quest*, four sizzling, action-packed romances in the tradition of *Romancing the Stone* and *The African Queen.* Starting in January 1994, one book each month is a sexy, romantic adventure focusing on the quest for passion…set against the essential elements of earth, wind, fire and water.

On sale in February

To banish the February blahs, there's *Wild Like the Wind* by Janice Kaiser. When her vengeful ex-husband kidnapped her beloved daughter Zara, Julia Powell hired Cole Bonner to rescue her. She was depending on the notorious mercenary's strength and stealth to free her daughter. What she hadn't counted on was the devastating effect of this wild and passionate man on *her*.

The quest continues…

Coming in March—*Aftershock* by Lynn Michaels
And in April—*Undercurrent* by Lisa Harris.

Passion's Quest—four fantastic adventures,
four fantastic love stories

AVAILABLE NOW: *Body Heat* by Elise Title (#473)

HARLEQUIN®
Temptation

HTPQ1

HARLEQUIN®

AMERICAN ◆ ROMANCE®

Meet four of the most mysterious, magical men…in

MORE
THAN
MEN

In January, make a date with Gabriel…
He had a perfect body, honey-brown hair and sea-blue eyes, and when
he rescued Gillian Aldair out of the crumbled mass of earth that was
an Andes landslide, Gillian swore she'd never seen a man quite like
him. But in her wildest imagination, she could never know just how
different Gabriel was.…

Join Rebecca Flanders for   **#517 FOREVER ALWAYS**
                              January 1994

Don't miss any of the MORE THAN MEN titles!

HARLEQUIN SUPERROMANCE ®

TIRED OF WINTER?
ESCAPE THE WINTER BLUES THIS SPRING WITH
HARLEQUIN SUPERROMANCE!

March is **Spring Break** month, and Superromance wants to give you a price break! Look for 30¢-off coupons in the back pages of all Harlequin Superromance novels, good on the purchase of your next Superromance title.

April Showers brings a shower of new authors! Harlequin Superromance is highlighting four simply sensational new authors. Four provocative, passionate, romantic stories guaranteed to put Spring into your heart!

May is the month for flowers, and with flowers comes **ROMANCE**! Join us in May as four of our most popular authors bring you four of their most romantic Superromance stories. Authors include Tracy Hughes, Janice Kaiser, Lynn Erickson and Bobby Hutchinson.

And to really escape the winter blues, enter our Superromantic Weekend Sweepstakes. Watch for further details in February Superromance novels.

HARLEQUIN SUPERROMANCE...
NOT THE SAME OLD STORY!

THE BABY IS ADORABLE...
BUT WHICH MAN IS HIS DADDY?

Alec Roman: He found baby Andy in a heart-shaped Valentine basket—but were finders necessarily keepers?

Jack Rourke: During his personal research into Amish culture, he got close to an Amish beauty—so close he thought he was the father.

Grady Noland: The tiny bundle of joy softened this rogue cop—and made him want to own up to what he thought were his responsibilities.

Cathy Gillen Thacker brings you TOO MANY DADS, a three-book series that asks the all-important question: Which man is about to become a daddy?

DADS